some girls are

Also by Courtney Summers

*Cracked Up to Be*

# some girls are

## courtney summers

St. Martin's Griffin   New York

SOME GIRLS ARE. Copyright © 2009 by Courtney Summers. All rights reserved.
Printed in the United States of America. For information, address St. Martin's Press, 175 Fifth Avenue, New York, N.Y. 10010.

www.stmartins.com

Library of Congress Cataloging-in-Publication Data

Summers, Courtney.
    Some girls are / Courtney Summers.—1st ed.
        p. cm.
    Summary: Regina, a high school senior in the popular—and feared—crowd, suddenly falls out of favor and becomes the object of the same sort of vicious bullying that she used to inflict on others, until she finds solace with one of her former victims.
    ISBN 978-0-312-57380-5
    [1. Bullies—Fiction.   2. Cliques (Sociology)—Fiction.   3. Emotional problems—Fiction.   4. High schools—Fiction.   5. Schools—Fiction.]   I. Title.
    PZ7.S95397So 2010
    [Fic]—dc22                                                                          2009033859

First Edition: January 2010

10   9   8   7   6   5   4   3   2   1

*To Amy Tipton and Lori Thibert*

*In Memory of Ken LaVallee*
*and Bob Summers*

# acknowledgments

Endless thanks to my agent, Amy Tipton, whose tireless guidance, support, and hard work on my behalf continues to make all of this possible. She's a force to be reckoned with and I aspire to her levels of fierceness. Sara Goodman, my editor, is a rock star who has an incredible way of looking at words, and her sharp insights inspire and make me a better writer. It's an honor to work with both of these amazing women and their endless passion and enthusiasm for this book saw it to its very last page.

To my family, David and Susan, Megan and Jarrad, Marion and Ken, Lucy and Bob and Damon, whose unconditional love and support means everything to me: Thank you with all of my heart. So much of this is what you gave to me.

Thanks to all at FinePrint Literary Management for being so awesome, particularly Stephany Evans, Colleen Lindsay, and Janet Reid. Thanks to all at St. Martin's Press for putting this book together and making the finished product look fantastic. Thanks to my brilliant copyeditor, Kate Davis, for catching all of my mistakes, and to my publicists, Katy Hershberger and Vimala Jeevanandam, who are absolutely fantastic at what they do.

Thanks to Lori Thibert, who has been a constant friend, support, and inspiration to me. There aren't enough words to describe what an incredible driving force she is, but I'm going to e-mail her to tell her how much she rocks after I finish this sentence. I honestly couldn't do it without her.

Many hearts and thanks to Baz, Kim, Samantha, and Whitney, a talented, fab, and sparkly four, who mean very much to me. They can always be counted on to bring the ~*~, and the ~*~ makes all the difference.

Many thanks to the wonderful Daisy Whitney—I'm in constant awe of her drive, her generosity, her kindness, and her time-management skills.

For their support and friendship and for being oh so cool (!), thanks to: Alicia R., Annika and Will K. Briony W., Carolyn M., Damon F., Danette H., Emily H., Fiona H., Jessica S., Kelvin T. and Tristan H., Laura S., Mehmet E., Mur L., Nova S., Susan A., Thomas T., Ursula D., Veronique M., Victoria S., and WMC.

Special thanks to Allie Costa for all the work she does and continues to do online in support of children's and YA authors everywhere and to all YA book bloggers, whose passion and enthusiasm for YA novels has created one of the best online communities out there. Special thanks also to Verla Kay's Blueboards for being one of the most helpful and supportive places for writers online (extra-special thanks to its moderators and administrators!).

And to absolutely everyone I've been fortunate enough to cross paths with both online and off since all of this began, who have given me their time, encouragement, kind words, and support: Thank you.

**Hallowell High:**

You're either someone or you're not.

I was someone. I was Regina Afton. I was Anna Morrison's best friend. These weren't small things, and despite what you may think, at the time they were worth keeping my mouth shut for.

Everyone is wasted.

Anna is wasted. Josh is wasted. Marta is wasted. Jeanette is wasted. Bruce is wasted. Donnie's always wasted. I'm not wasted. I had my turn at the last party, called shotgun in Anna's Benz after it was over. My head was out the window, the world was spinning. I puked my guts out. It wasn't fun, but it's not like there was anything else to do. Tonight, there's even less to do than that. Tonight, I'm the designated driver.

Boring.

"Okay, okay, just—" Josh fumbles into his pocket and pulls out a little baggie of capsules. He tips one, two, three, four into his palm while Charlie Simmons, a fat, cranky sophomore, waits impatiently. "I have to restock." He drops the pills into Charlie's piggy hands. "That's all I can give you right now, man."

Charlie sniffs. Fitting: All that Adderall is going up his nose.

"How much?"

"Oh . . ." Josh's eyes glaze over. "Forget about it. I like you, Chuck."

Charlie grins. "Cool. Thanks."

"Hey, *Chuck*, you're paying," I say, grabbing his arm. Instant scowl. "Bring the money on Monday."

"Bitch," he mutters.

He stalks off. Payment secured. I only strong-arm Josh's clientele when Josh gives his merchandise away, which is every time he gets this drunk.

"Jesus, Regina." He somehow manages to trip over his feet, even though he's just standing there. He wraps an arm around me. "Show a little respect, huh?"

"Fuck Charlie Simmons."

He laughs, and the ability to remain upright completely abandons him, forcing all his weight on me. I struggle to keep us standing, casting my gaze around the property for help. The lights are on, the music's loud, and I spot a few people puking in the topiary, but none of them are my friends.

Josh buries his head into my neck. "You look hot tonight." His blond hair tickles my face, and I push him back. It's too hot out to be this close. "I mentioned that, right?"

"Let's go inside," I tell him.

He laughs again, like *Let's go inside* is code for something it's not, but I guess he's right: I guess I look hot tonight. Anna loaned me a shirt and skirt, and everything she owns is nice. *I want you to look really good for once, Regina.* I've spent the last seven hours afraid someone's going to vomit all over me, because I can't afford to replace the labels I'm wearing.

I help Josh up the path to his front door. He stops abruptly, opens his arms wide, and shouts, "Is everybody having a good time?"

He's met with scattered applause and cheers that barely make it over the music. He shakes his head ruefully, listing sideways. I wonder what would happen if I just let him fall this time, but he manages to regain his balance without my help.

"We're graduating in like, eight months," he tells me very seriously. "I'm going to *Yale.* Who will supply these poor kids while I'm gone?"

I roll my eyes and right him for the thousandth time, forcing him into the house, where it's a different kind of party-chaos—quieter, but just as corrupt. Music filters in from outside, clashing with the music playing inside. Four seniors are toking up at the kitchen table. Drinking games. People making out in the living room. It's boring—it always is—but it's all there is. I just wish I was trashed enough to be able to pretend to enjoy it. I *hate* being designated driver. It was Kara's turn this time, but she's at home, sick.

"Are we going upstairs?" Josh asks when we reach the stairs. Before I can answer, he crumples onto the steps in a heap, too heavy for me to pick up. He rolls onto his back and blinks twice, struggling to focus. "Is this my bedroom?"

"Yes," I lie.

I bend down and kiss his cheek.

The smoke wafting in from the kitchen is giving me a headache, or maybe it's the music—I don't know. I lean against the wall and check my watch. It's officially Too Late, but Anna says the designated driver doesn't get to decide when the party is over; everyone else gets to decide when they're over the party. And Anna—I lost her an hour ago. Her face was as red as her hair, and she was slobbering all over Donnie.

I sigh.

Jeanette lurches up from out of nowhere looking like a guaranteed good time. Strung out. I can never tell when she's over the party; the party's usually all over her.

"I'm leaving," she declares. "With Henry."

"Is Henry sober?"

"Yes, he is," Henry says in my ear, startling me. He grins and points to Josh, sprawled out on the stairs. "You can't just leave him there."

I ignore him and turn to her. "Where's Marta?"

"Waiting in the car." She brushes her hair out of her eyes. "We're dropping her off at her house, and then me and Henry are going back to his place."

"Is Henry sober?"

"I'm right here," Henry says, annoyed. "And you already asked that."

"Do you *really* want to go to his place?" I ask Jeanette. Another of my duties as designated driver. If I can't prevent an undesirable drunken hookup, then why bother being here sober in the first place? Jeanette grins and nods.

"You know, I'm in the circle," Henry points out. "I get an automatic pass."

"But you're kind of an asshole," I tell him.

He smirks and laces his fingers through Jeanette's. They amble through the smoke. He glances back at me once. "Have fun babysitting, Afton."

Josh on the stairs. Marta in the car. Henry taking her home. Henry taking Jeanette back to his place. I don't care about Bruce, so that just leaves Anna and Donnie. I know they're in the den. They always end up in the den if Josh and I don't get there first. The den is off-limits.

But we're in the circle.

I bypass the living-room festivities, open the door to the den, step inside, and close it behind me. The party noises fade and the room is dim, moonlight slivering in through the curtain drawn over the glass doors that lead to the backyard. I close my eyes briefly, inhaling slowly, letting the semiquiet of it all kill my headache.

When I open my eyes, I spot Anna at one end of the room. She's curled up on the couch, a picture of six shots of Jack chased with one Heineken too many. She drinks too much around Donnie, desperate to keep up with him, like the difference between him staying with her and leaving her is her blood-alcohol level.

"I need a girlfriend who can hold her liquor," he says.

Maybe it is. Donnie's lounging in the chair at the opposite end of the room, looking as half awake as he always does. No matter how hard I try, I can't seem to talk Anna out of him. He has a *convertible*.

She'd kill me if I left her here like this, so I lean over her ear and say her name, loud and sharp: "Anna." She doesn't move. I pull on her arm, tap her face, shake her. Nothing. I make my way over to the pitcher of water sitting on the end table beside Donnie.

"Help me get her to the car," I say.

He stares at me. "Why? Where are you going?"

"Home."

"What about me? I'm in no condition to get myself back to my place."

"I don't care what happens to you. I'm going home and I'm taking Anna with me." I grab the water and pour a glass, cross the room, and try to get her upright enough to take a sip, somehow. "Anna, come on . . ."

She flops back on the couch. I rub my forehead—my headache's returning—and make my way back to Donnie with the glass.

"Would you give me a hand?" He stares at me and then grabs my arm. The water sloshes onto the table. "*Christ*, Donnie."

He keeps his hand on my arm, and I'm suddenly aware of how much skin Anna's shirt isn't covering, but I guess that's the point.

"Why don't you care what happens to me?"

He sounds as pathetic as he looks.

"God, you're drunk." I step back, but he keeps his hand on my arm. "Just crash here," I say. "I'm not driving you home." He digs his nails into my skin. I yank his hand off me. "Don't."

"Don't," he repeats in a soft falsetto, and then he grabs my other arm before I can move, gripping them both so tightly, I know I'll still feel his fingers tomorrow. He uses me to get to his feet, and then he's on his feet and he's close.

Too close.

I turned him down in the ninth grade. Anna likes to say we've been close to hate-fucking ever since, which is too gross for me to even contemplate. It's a gunshot kind of thing for her to say—a warning. The way she says it, it's like she can see it happening, and the way she says it lets me know I better not let it happen.

As if I'd ever let Donnie get that close to me, anyway.

Except now he's that close to me, and I think he's thinking the wrong things.

He is. He presses his mouth against mine, mashing my lips against my teeth. The inevitability of every party: Someone will kiss you and you won't want it. Except this is worse than that. Way, way worse. This is my best friend's boyfriend, and my best friend is passed out on a couch eight feet away, and she will kill me for this, and I really, *really* don't want it. I press my hands against his chest and push him back, trying to force *stop* out of my mouth and past his. He detaches himself and fumbles backward. I wipe my mouth on the back of my hand, trying to get the taste of him out. I need water. I need to spit. He grabs my arm. I try to jerk away, but he holds fast.

"You better not breathe a *word* about this to her—"

"Donnie, fuck off."

He keeps tightening his grip until I can't keep the pain off my face—it hurts—so I bring my foot down on his foot and watch that happen on *his* face. It bursts red and I'm free. I rush to the door, but before I can open it, he's on me, crushing me into place from behind and breathing so hard in my ear, I can't even hear the vague sounds of the music outside or in. What turns a moment into this—me against the door, him against me. He puts his hand on my shoulder and turns me around roughly, and I'm afraid.

I've never been afraid of Donnie Henderson before.

He forces another kiss on me, lips working overtime, trying to get something out of mine. I grab a fistful of his hair and pull. He shoves me, but I stumble past him. The brief space I put between us makes me think it'll be okay, that this is as out of hand as it gets, but it's too close or it's not close enough and he lunges for me and we both go down.

We're on the floor.

He pushes me into the carpet. I glimpse Anna, tangled red hair, eyes closed. *Anna, wake up.* What turns a moment into this—he's on top of me, panting, and my face is smashed against the rug. I focus on the strands of hair laid gently across Anna's face.

This isn't happening.

But he turns me over and slides his hand up my skirt, and this is really really really really happening.

"No—"

I reach out and grip one of the table legs. His hand up my skirt. One hand up my skirt. Touching me. And the other clumsily feeling every part of me it can. His mouth on my neck. I yank the leg. The table tips and the pitcher rolls off, vomiting water all over us. Wet. Hands all over me.

I grab the pitcher and bring it up and then down on him. It's hardly a hit, but he feels it. I raise it up again and he dodges me and I'm crawling away. Last shot, Regina. *Get out.* I grab the chair and pull myself to my feet while he tries to stand, but the last of his coordination is gone on his hand up my skirt. Anna's skirt.

"Anna!" I turn to her. "Anna, help!"

But she just lays there, and Donnie's blocking my path to the door, swearing, trying to stand, and my heart is trying to race me out of this room before that happens. I stumble over to the sliding glass door and yank it open. I step outside, into the heat, into the party, the last of the party, but the music is as loud as it was at the start of the night.

I need to tell someone, but everyone is wasted.

I walk fast. I walk forever, blind, numb. I wrap my arms around myself. I need to tell someone. I lick my lips and taste salt: I'm crying. How long have I been—

Kara.

I'm standing in front of Kara's house. My feet walked me here. Kara. Kara is someone. The walk to her door sets off the motion sensor, soaking me in artificial too-bright light. I knock and wait, fighting the urge to throw up. I wipe my eyes and pull at Anna's skirt. It's torn.

A minute later, the door opens. Kara's there, a fevered doll with blond curls hanging in front of her flushed face. She crinkles her snotty nose.

"Jesus, Regina. What part of 'designated driver' don't you understand?"

The contempt in her voice almost tricks me into feeling normal. For a second. And then she looks closer and I remember the skirt—Anna's skirt—and his hand up Anna's skirt. And I'm still crying.

"What happened to you?" she asks.

A million words fight their way up my throat, all lobbying to be first out of my mouth. They pile up, stuck. Only one manages its way out: "Help."

She lets me inside, and the rest of the words come, falling from my lips, a stupid, stuttering truth. By the time I collapse in a chair at the kitchen table, she knows what he did to me. And then it gets really quiet while I wait for her to tell me what to do.

I need someone to tell me what to do.

Anna always tells me what to do.

"God," Kara murmurs, pressing her fingers against the angry spots on my arm where he grabbed me. The skin is tender and marked, but by Monday it will be splotchy purples, browns, and yellows.

"The police?" I ask. My voice cracks. "Do you think? Do I go to the police?"

Kara stares at me, and then she stands and goes into the fridge and gets a bottle of water. I can't read her expression.

"You really want to put yourself through that?"

"I could put Donnie through that." I rub my forehead. But I don't really want to go through that. I don't want to talk to the police about his hand up my skirt. And then—my parents. It's not like you can do that and not tell your parents, and I don't want them to know. I don't want them to think of me on the floor, with Donnie's hands there. Kara sets the water in front of me. "Maybe Anna—"

"You're going to tell *Anna*?"

"She has to know—" I swallow. "That's her boyfriend. She won't let him get away with it." She'll take care of him. Me. She takes care of everything.

"If she believes you."

I open my mouth and nothing comes out. *If she believes you.* I should've known Kara would do this. There's a reason we hate each other. *If she believes you.*

"Look, *I* believe you," Kara says, reading my mind. "I know you hate Donnie, and I can see him doing something like this, but . . . Anna's always thought . . ."

*You're like, this close to hate-fucking.*

I pick at the hem of Anna's skirt. The jagged rip in it finally hits me. She'll kill me. She will kill me for ruining her skirt. "Shit." I stand and try to force the ragged sides together, like that's how you fix these things. "I need to—I told her I'd be careful—"

"Regina—"

"I told Anna I wouldn't—"

*"Regina."* She snaps her fingers twice. I let the skirt go and sink back into the chair. I need to get it together. Kara stares at me, concerned. I never thought I'd live a moment that could exist outside our hate for each other. I could go my whole life without one. But this feels . . . safe.

"What do you—so what do I do, Kara? What . . . ?"

She sits across from me, quiet, for a long time. My stomach knots itself up while I wait for her to speak. If I have to live with this, I don't want it to be hard.

"Donnie's not going to tell Anna," she finally says. "And Anna's not going to believe Donnie would do that to you. She'd think you were screwing around behind her back. It's not fair, but that's Anna."

My best friend.

"I mean . . ." She taps her fingers along the table. "He was really wasted, right? It's not like he does that all the time. . . ." I don't say anything. "And I feel really bad for you, Regina . . . but there are some things worth keeping your mouth shut for."

"She's my best friend." A tear manages its way down my cheek. I wipe at my eyes. "I mean—"

"But you know what she'd do to you if she found out, right?"

I nod slowly. I know. And then I nod again: *I know, I know, I know.*

"And I'm totally here for you," she says. Kara. Totally here. Nothing makes sense anymore. "I'm not going to say anything."

"Thanks," I whisper.

Kara presses her fingers against my arm again.

Her touch is cool and strange.

I wake up, and the bruises on my arms have turned really yellow and brown, so I have to wear long sleeves, even though fall is doing its best impression of summer and the air is sticky and hot. Anna decided we'll all wear tank tops and miniskirts for as long as the weather holds—before winter confines us to less revealing outfits—and I agreed, so I don't know what I'll tell her when she sees me today and asks what my deal is.

And I'll have to tell her something, because I can't tell her the truth.

I debate various lies over breakfast, a pale pink antacid with coffee. I'm a pretty good liar as long as I'm talking to an easy sell, but Anna is not an easy sell. If she finds out I'm hiding something, she'll want to know what. Maybe she'll be mad. Maybe she won't give a damn. Anna is funny like that.

I decide to tell her I'm having a fat day.

"Little warm out for that shirt, isn't it, Regina?" Mom asks, setting a plate of eggs and toast in front of Dad. Her comment draws his eyes up from the paper.

"You'll melt," he says.

I shrug and drain my coffee. "Whatever. I'll see you later."

Halfway to school, I feel like I'm going to throw up. I fan my face with my hand, and the air that meets my skin is hot. My shirt clings to my back, pressed uncomfortably into place by my book bag. A pay phone looms on the horizon, the closest thing I've got to a cell phone, because my parents kind of suck. I drop my bag and rifle through my pockets for change until I find a quarter. I use it to call Josh.

*Pick up, Josh. Pick up.* I imagine the song that plays when someone calls his cell, exploding from his pocket until he picks up, but he never does, which is weird because Josh always picks up, and he's always good for a ride. He's my boyfriend.

**Hallowell High: The** parking lot pulses with scantily clad life, and I'm in the middle of it all, wearing a sweater. My scraggly black hair is plastered to my forehead, and a couple people point and stare at me because I look that ridiculous, but I don't care. I'm still better than them. It's not hard. Hallowell is one of those in-between towns, stuck between a city and another city, and everyone here knows everyone else. It's too small for a social landscape more complicated than this: You're either someone or you're not.

I'm someone.

I'm Regina Afton. I'm Anna Morrison's best friend. These aren't small things, and Kara's right: They're worth keeping my mouth shut for. So I kept my mouth shut the whole weekend, and I'm still Regina Afton and I'm still Anna Morrison's best friend.

Friday never happened.

I wipe a light sheen of sweat from my forehead. Anna, Kara, Jeanette, and Marta usually wait for me at the front so we can enter school the Fearsome Fivesome. It's the only part of the day I sort of like, standing next to Anna, untouchable.

Everyone is afraid of us.

Today, they're nowhere to be found.

I scope out the parking lot just in time to see a black convertible pull in. Donnie. My stomach twists and I can't breathe. I feel wrong in all the wrong places. I have to get inside. Now. I navigate the cacophony of voices, drug deals and insults—

"—See you at lunch, okay?—"

"—I didn't finish it, but I don't think Bradbury will care—"

"—Wait up, I've got to get—"

"—For one pill? Fuck you! I can get them cheaper from—"

"—Slut! HEY, SLUT—"

—and push through the front doors, into the air-conditioned main corridor. I scan the halls. They can't be that far off. I just need to find them. I feel naked without them.

A flash of blond hair catches my eye.

"Kara!" She doesn't turn around. She must not have heard me. *"Kara!"*

She stops and I hurry over. Being next to her calms me a little; I'm not invincible yet, but it's better than nothing. And it's weird. I never thought we could be friendly, but she was nice to me. So I'll be nice to her. For a while.

"Have you seen Anna?"

But she stares at me like I've just told her to stab her eyes out with a pen, and even though she gives me that look a lot, I don't get it today.

"Uh, yeah?" Bitch-voice. Okay.

I readjust my book bag and clear my throat.

"Where is she? I want to talk to her. She called this weekend and I didn't pick up." I wasn't ready. "You know Anna. She'll be pissed."

"Yeah," Kara agrees. "You could say that."

"What? Did you talk to her?"

Kara shrugs and flounces down the hall, her golden curls bouncing off her shoulders as she goes. A bitter taste works its way up my throat in spite of the antacid I took. I follow her. She turns a corner. I turn it.

Jeanette and Marta are at Marta's locker. Kara prances over, and they enfold her into our secret huddle, the one I should be at the heart of, but my feet are cemented into place by some kind of animal instinct that tells me I'm not allowed over there. Marta spots me. My heart leaps. *Invite me over.* She murmurs something to the other girls. *Invite me over.* They laugh. *Invite me over.*

They turn their backs to me. No.

No way.

This is not a freeze-out.

## But I have to find Anna to be sure.

She's not at her locker. I check her homeroom. She's not there either. I stalk the halls, and people are looking at me, whispering. But it's the sweater.

I detour into the girls' washroom, not because I think Anna will be there, but because my stomach is upset. I pop two more antacids and lean over the sink. My heart spazzes in my chest and my arms itch. I scratch along the outside of my sweater because I don't want to look at the bruises, even though I could close my eyes and see them.

I could close my eyes and see—

*Don't think about it. Don't think about it. Don't think about it.*

I stare at my reflection in the mirror. My hair is limp, dead, and my face is an unattractive overheated red. Anna would not approve. Anna doesn't want to talk to me because . . . Because. Because.

I haven't returned her clothes yet.

I ignored her all weekend.

Duh.

Anna doesn't want to talk to me, and the other girls are giving me the Cryptic Cold Shoulder until I apologize to her. I exhale. It's almost comforting in its familiarity. I've been here before and I can handle it. It's not fun, but it's easy.

It's not a freeze-out.

I'll find her. Apologize.

The first bell rings. Homeroom. I haven't even gotten my books. I leave the washroom and step into the hall, forcing my way past the whispers and stares.

It's the sweater. That's all it is.

And then I push through the crowd converged in front of my locker so I can get a good look at the word spray-painted across it.

## WHORE

This is a freeze-out.

The scene fades out until it's me and that word and nothing else.

I step forward and touch my fingers to one of the letters. It comes back black. I rub my sleeve across the metal. The paint is fresh enough to ruin my shirt but dry enough to keep from smearing into an unintelligible mess.

"Is it true?" Someone asks. I touch the paint again. It's really there. "Did you really bone Donnie Henderson?"

The scene fades back in. Voices assert themselves over the sound of my heart pounding in my chest, and they're all saying something about me.

Me. Donnie Henderson. Did I really bone Donnie Henderson.

His hand up my skirt. Mouth on my neck.

I step back and end up on someone's foot. They swear at me. *Watch it, bitch.* I focus on not looking like a cornered animal and try to zero in on a face I know, someone familiar amid the slack-jawed rubberneckers.

Josh. My boyfriend.

He hovers just outside the mob. Our eyes meet.

He turns away.

"Oh, my *God*, here comes Holt." Another voice. "This is *so awe-some!*"

The second bell rings. Principal Holt is there before I can escape, the decrepit old janitor trailing behind him. His face purples as he surveys the damage. He paces, yells, and makes such a fuss, a new crowd is born. He orders a temporary cover for my locker until the paint can be removed, and he vows the perpetrators will be brought to justice.

And then he asks me if I know who they are.

After homeroom, I'm gone. I'm at that pay phone again and I'm calling Josh. Again. I pick at the phone book dangling from a string, half torn away by some vandal with nothing better to do, while the sun continues its slow rise overhead. It's hot in this booth. I turn my back to the cars rushing past me, on their way to the main street.

I finally get his voice mail.

"It's me." A car goes by. I swallow twice and try to figure out what to say while the silence on the other end of the line waits for me to fill it. "Look, what they're—what they're all saying—what I—" I can't tell this to Josh. Not on the phone. ". . . You heard it from Kara, didn't you?"

I hang up. Kara.

Kara, Kara, Kara.

Kara Myers.

*Kara.*

I am such a fool.

I'm used to everyone's eyes on me; that's nothing new. When you're Anna Morrison's best friend, people look. We're the kind of popular that parents like to pretend doesn't exist so they can sleep at night, and we're the kind of popular that makes our peers unable to sleep at night. Everyone hates us, but they're afraid of us, too. Anna thrives on it. She says the day people stop hating us is the day something is really wrong. She says I should look at it that way, but I can't. Everyone hates us, and it makes me a total wreck.

She hated that about me.

*These people are* nothing. *They don't matter. None of this matters. There's a whole world outside of this hellhole. God, Regina. You could at least act like you don't give a damn.*

So I do it like she does it: I square my shoulders and march across the parking lot, my jaw clenched and my eyes narrowed. I try not to let the heat touch me or flinch at the blast of cold air on my skin when I step through the school doors.

I'm ushered in by whispers and stares. Half the student body relishes it; they've waited a long time to show me just how much they hate me. The other half doesn't know what to make of it after spending four years fearfully revering me.

Principal Holt makes quick work of restoring my locker, but whoever repainted it doesn't know how to color-match. My locker has been painted red. Every other locker in this school is a bright, hideous pumpkin orange. It's a wash of a coat, too.

I can still see the WHORE forcing its way through.

I grab my books. Two girls go by, and I hear my name but not the context surrounding it. Probably something like: *Regina Afton is a slut who slept with Anna Morrison's boyfriend I know can you believe it pass it on.*

I will kill myself before I get used to this.

Anna catches my eye then, swaggering down the hall in the opposite direction. A dozen guys watch her as she goes; it's the way her skirt moves with her hips when she walks. She takes a sharp turn left, and I know where she's going. And she's alone.

This is my chance.

I take the same left, push through the pale blue door that opens into the girls' washroom, and there she is, admiring her reflection in the mirrors over the sinks. I don't blame her. Anna is beautiful, with her soft, fine auburn hair and the kind of body that brings guys to their knees. It's cliché, but she's a Siren. Impossible to fight, there's no better feeling than to hear her sing your name until she has you and eats you alive. The people at this school think it's hard enough living beneath her, but it's even harder being her friend. Anna.

The door swings shut. She stiffens and turns, and the air leaves my lungs. I'm torn between wanting to be far away from her and wanting to throw myself at her feet to beg forgiveness for something I didn't do. As long as it means we can be friends again.

*I'm sorry. I'll never sleep with your boyfriend again, never, never, never. . . .*

Maybe I should've thought this out better.

She takes me in slowly, one eyebrow arched. She wants me to feel like I'm not good enough to be acknowledged, and it's working. I'm suddenly aware of the sloppy ponytail tied at the back of my head and how dumb my outfit looks—jeans and a sweater on another sweltering day—but it doesn't matter. She's always been prettier than me.

"Nice job you did on my locker," I say.

We stare at each other, Western-movie-showdown–style. Several agonizing seconds pass, but Anna never draws her gun, which is good, because I'm totally unarmed. She turns back to the mirror and digs through the makeup bag in front of her.

"I didn't do it." She pulls out some lip gloss. "I had it done."

"I didn't have sex with him, Anna."

"Wow," she says. "You almost sound like you mean it."

"Kara's lying to you. She set me up—"

She snorts. "Don't even."

"She *is*. She set me up. You know she hates my guts—"

"How dumb do you think I am, Regina? You know the part that really makes me sick?" She tilts her chin up, eyes never straying from her reflection. "I was *right there*. Did you get off on that?"

"Anna, he—" The words come out of my mouth fast and stupid, because if I think about them too much, I won't be able to say them. "Anna, he tried to rape me—"

It doesn't go over well. She slams the gloss down and whirls around, her face as red as her hair.

"I cannot *believe* you just said that."

This is the air sucked out of my lungs, this is a punch in the stomach, this is a slap across the face, and *that* is *not* what she was supposed to say.

"I'm your best friend," I choke out.

"You were until you fucked my boyfriend."

"Anna, I *didn't*."

She drops the gloss back into her bag. "I've been saying it forever. You always acted like you hated him, and you tried every trick in the book to get me to break up with him, and when that didn't work, you waited. Now you're caught and you're scared and you're standing there telling me he tried to *rape* you? That is *fucked*, Regina."

"Wait—I'll show—I'll show you—"

I'll show her the bruises. I fumble with my sleeves, my hands shaking horribly, while Anna zips up her bag. The washroom door swings open, interrupting me, and when I turn around, it's Kara. She looks so different. Like, confident.

So this is really bad.

"Bell's gonna go," she says over me. "Are you coming?"

I turn back to Anna. She smiles at me. No, not *at* me—through me. She's smiling at Kara, through me, but this can't be over because I haven't had my say. In the movies, you get the time to make the speech that saves your life, and everyone wants to listen to you. She hasn't even seen the bruises yet.

"Anna, just wait—"

"Yeah," Anna says to Kara, over me. "Let's go."

"Anna—"

"You hear something?" Kara asks Anna, grinning.

"Anna, please." Anna gives herself one last look in the mirror, grabs her makeup bag, and passes me on her way out. The air that follows her smells berry sweet, and I beg after it. "Anna, Anna, *Anna*—"

"Fuck off, Regina," she says in a singsong voice.

And she leaves.

Kara doesn't. I feel her behind me; I feel every part of her enjoying this. I take Anna's place in front of the mirror, trying to ignore how sick it makes me that every part of Kara is enjoying this. I try to conjure the Regina she was afraid of. The one who put her in her place. Over and over again.

I can't.

"You talked me out of it." My voice breaks. "You told me not to tell."

"Well, it wouldn't have done *me* any good if you had," she says in that same singsong voice that Anna used, and then she leaves, and I bite my lip until I taste blood.

It hurts less than what just happened here.

For the first time in four years at this school, I'm aware of the cafeteria like I've never been aware of it before. Greasy, overcrowded, hot and loud.

I can see *everyone*.

Those teen movies that use the cafeteria to present the social hierarchies of high school, the ones where the lunch tables become little islands, spaces for you and people like you and no one else, where the overlap is nonexistent—they're all wrong. Hallowell High's cafeteria is *only* overlap. Cliques bleed into other cliques for lack of space, and there's only one exception: Anna's table. It's always been Anna and everyone else.

And now me.

This must be what the first day of ninth grade felt like for people who didn't have seating insurance. I scan rows of tables for an empty chair, but my gaze keeps drifting back to home base, where there are two—mine and Donnie's.

They're all watching me.

Fourteen pairs of eyes track this moment where I'm lost and it's obvious. I maneuver around tables with as much purpose as I can muster, pretending I've got somewhere to be until I find somewhere to be. I end up at the table at the back, the one next to the long line of garbage cans. It's the Garbage Table. It's Michael Hayden's table. It's nearly always empty because no one likes eating next to the garbage.

No one likes eating next to Michael Hayden.

He's hunched over a burger and Coke, writing in the Moleskine he's constantly carrying around. Michael Hayden: Unstable Emo Writer Boy.

I pick at my fingernails and debate how to do this. Michael probably doesn't want me to sit with him. We have phys ed together and I'm sure that's enough of me for him. It's enough of him for me, but when I look up, he's watching me. My face gets hot, but I go all fake-confidence on him and walk over. He closes the notebook and shoves it aside.

"Can I sit here?"

He doesn't say anything. Doesn't look at me. I decide it's an invitation and sit. I pick my nails while he eats. I don't actually eat lunch in the traditional sense; I dig into my pockets and pull out a pill. Everyone's eyes are on me. I can't imagine what they're thinking. This is Michael—longish, dark brown hair that always hangs into his pale blue eyes. His face is all sharp features, and he's tall, broad shoulders, sort of built. He moved here during ninth grade, when his shrink mother decided to set up a practice in town. He came here quiet—not shy, but removed, above it all. Like he just didn't care about us.

We tried to make him care. It didn't work. So first we told everyone he was a creep. Stay away. We couldn't even give a solid reason why, but because it came from Anna's mouth, that was good enough. He was a freak, and then his mother died in the eleventh grade and Anna was thrilled; she finally had a solid reason.

Michael now: We got everyone to believe his mom's death made him snap, and he's a torturing-small-animals kind of walking anger-management problem, that he's on meds, and his Moleskine holds school-shooting manifestos.

So this is going to be awkward.

I swallow the antacid dry. My throat is tight and it refuses to go down. I try again. The pill begins a slow dissolve over my tongue. I finally dredge up enough spit to force the thing down. The clock on the wall behind Michael's head tells me there are twenty minutes of lunch period left. I'm not obligated to wait them out here, but a small part of me wants to do it to prove that I can.

Michael steadfastly ignores me, radiating the kind of tension that makes me want to go in on myself and stay there, until he finally looks at me and then past me.

"They're watching you," he says.

"I didn't sleep with him," I say. I don't know why. "Donnie, I mean."

He stares at me like he clearly doesn't give a fuck and wants to know why I think he should. It's the kind of look that makes me feel every inch of my skin in a way that makes me want to claw it all off.

He hates me.

I twist around in my chair. The seven heads turned in my direction go back to their food, whispering. I can just guess what they're saying.

"So how come they're telling everyone you did?"

"I got set up." I say it casually, but I feel every word in my gut, and it causes the kind of upset a pill can't reach. "By someone who I thought was my friend."

Except Kara was never my friend. She was just one of those girls you have to throw a bone to because there's nowhere else for them to go, and you've known them for so long, you can't even remember how you met.

"Kara," I tell him, even though he didn't ask. Saying her name elicits a Pavlovian response from me. My hands twitch, overcome with the urge to strangle her to death.

"I guess that's what you get," he says.

Our eyes meet. He stares at me, and I can only take it for a second before I have to look away.

He looks like his mom.

"She used to be really fat," he says. "Kara."

"Your point?"

He shrugs. I know what he's implying. I don't care. It's no secret.

Everyone knows Kara used to be fat until the second half of tenth grade, when she learned how to stick her fingers down her throat and started popping diet pills. She had to wear a wig in her class photo because she was losing her hair; you can see it if you look really closely. It was the pills or the purging. And those were only suggestions, anyway.

It's not like I told her she *had* to do that to herself.

Michael goes back to his burger. I try not to watch him eat, but I end up watching him eat anyway. It always amazes me how people can relax enough in this place to do that—eat—and not care. He finishes it off with precious minutes of the period to spare. He uses those to study me, and I get that claw-my-skin-off feeling. I know he's trying to make me feel so uncomfortable I won't come back and sit here . . .

Tomorrow.

I have to do this all over again tomorrow.

"I knew your mom," I blurt out.

He blinks, surprised. I've surprised him. And then his eyes light up in the strangest way—like he hasn't heard the word *mom* in a long time. It's not exactly happy, it's sort of curious—like, *Mom. I know that word.*

"How?" he demands.

"We—" For a second my head is full of her office, the way it smelled—sort of like coffee—and the walls were this pale blue. Her voice was soft and kind. "We were friends."

I feel bad for the lie, but it's not like I don't want it to be true. I don't know if his mom ever thought of me as anything but her patient, but I really liked her and I wish we had been friends. It's horrible, but sometimes I'm relieved she died before she could ever find out what I helped do to her son.

"She never mentioned you," he says.

"We were friends," I repeat. He searches my face for the lie. I sweat it out until he concedes and says, "Maybe."

The bell rings.

"Can I sit here with you tomorrow?" I ask. It's humiliating having to ask permission to sit at the Garbage Table, and when he doesn't answer me immediately, I pose the question again with the kind of urgency that makes me sound totally pathetic. "Michael, can I sit here with you tomorrow at lunch?"

"What if I said no?" he asks. My mouth goes dry. *You can't.* The cafeteria is emptying. Ms. Nelson stands by the door, waiting for the last of us to leave, but I can't leave without this one thing and he knows it. "Regina, I don't care where you sit."

He grabs his things, gets up, and makes his way out. I stay, staring at the table until Nelson blows her whistle and tells me to "get out there."

*BITCH.*

Kara drops the note on my desk on her way to the board to do a few math problems for Mr. Brenner, and her wrist action is so subtle, he doesn't even see it and he's looking right at her. And that has everything to do with how short her skirt is.

I crush the note into a neat little ball.

"Well done," Brenner says, as Kara chalks down the answers to the last problem. He's staring at her legs like the skeeve he is.

Bruce waves his hand around.

"Excuse me, sir? I did the problems with Kara, and she got the last one wrong."

The silence is delicious. Kara reddens and Brenner blinks, totally caught.

"Maybe *you* got it wrong, Burton," he suggests, and waits for the rest of the class to laugh, like, *Yeah, maybe.*

We don't.

"I doubt it, sir," Bruce says.

*That's* when we laugh. Brenner tells us to be quiet, and we review the problem as a class, and sure enough, Kara got it wrong, so Brenner has to backtrack. He starts babbling about the "mathematical journey" and how the steps you take are sometimes more important than the destination, until he loses his ridiculous train of thought and sends Kara back to her seat.

I stare at the crumpled note, and when she's close enough, I wind my arm back and whip it at her forehead. She shrieks and Brenner totally sees it, so it's detention for me, shelving returns in the library after school.

There's no such thing as justice.

I'm in the library wedging a copy of *Flowers in the Attic* between two copies of *Persuasion* when Liz Cooper and Charie Andrews come in. Proof positive a bad day can always get worse. I back into the narrow shelves until I'm out of sight and they pass by, talking low, and end up in the stacks directly behind me. Charie is a total no one, but Liz is this faded-out yellow-haired girl-ghost I've gone to elaborate lengths to avoid because being around her makes my stomach ache. I reach into my pocket and force an antacid between my lips, chewing it in hopes that will make it work faster.

They're talking about me, of course. I'd be shocked if they weren't. I get as close to the books as I can and hope they don't see me spying on them through the shelves. I don't even know why I'm eavesdropping. They won't say anything I want to hear.

"Donnie didn't even show today," Charie is saying.

"He's probably out getting wasted," Liz replies, and she's probably right. For Donnie, sobriety is a fate worse than his inevitable death from liver failure.

"Did you see her looking for somewhere to sit at lunch? It was totally hilarious. I kept hoping she'd come over and ask if she could sit with you."

"Why?"

"So you could tell her no." Charie laughs because it's *totally hilarious*. Liz doesn't laugh, but I almost wish she would. It's always easier when the people you've ruined decide to really hate you—like Michael does—because then your defenses go up and you can't even really feel the bad things you've done.

"She sat with Michael," Liz says.

"He's too nice." Charie's voice is all disappointment. "I caught up with him in history and asked him if she was really upset, but he said she seemed normal. It has to be a front, though, right? She gets kicked out of her clique and they all hate her and Josh dumped her—" I jerk back. I don't remember that part happening. ". . . She'll be slitting her wrists soon enough."

I swallow. I swallow again. I don't know what feels worse: Josh breaking up with me *without breaking up with me*, Charie joking about my suicide, or Liz's gentle admonition of it—"Charie, don't."

"Hey, it could happen," Charie says. "Anyway, I've got to catch Paul. See you."

"See you."

Charie flits by my shelves. I wait while Liz rifles through book after book after book. After a while, she settles at a table nearby and opens up a paperback. I lean against the shelf and close my eyes. I'm trapped here until she leaves. Facing her is not an option.

"Regina," she says, and my heart stops. I open my eyes and she's staring in my direction. "I know you're there. You can come out."

I step out slowly. She looks me over, starting at my feet and working her way up to my eyes. I have to force myself to hold her gaze. I don't like looking Liz in the eyes. It's stupid, but I'm afraid I'll see her like the last time I really saw her. Totally broken. I mean, I still see that on her—everyone does. It'll be all over her until she graduates.

But I'm afraid I'll see it now like I saw it then.

"Aren't you going to say anything?" I ask her.

"What would I have to say to you?"

"I just thought you'd enjoy this, is all."

"That still doesn't mean I'd have anything to say to you."

The moment should end here, but I'm rooted to the spot. I stare at the literacy poster tacked on the wall behind her head. "Read or die." I feel like I should be saying something important, but the chance for that has passed. A long time ago.

"The locker was impressive," she says. "What do you think they'll do next?"

"I don't know," I say. "Guess you'll have to tune in to find out."

She closes her book. "Well, I'm here every day. But I don't know, it's kind of boring. I've seen this show before. I totally starred in it once. Remember?"

A familiar, horrible feeling consumes me. I want to tell her it wasn't easy for me, either, watching Anna torture her every day until the light in her eyes went out. I want to tell her, but that would be dumb.

"Got any tips?" I try to keep my voice light.

She laughs a little. It's been ages since I heard her laugh and mean it, and even though it's at my expense, and for a minute it's so familiar it's like we're in her room, giggling about things that don't mean any-thing, a really happy moment until Anna would call her cell phone, looking for me.

"Good luck, Regina," Liz says. "You'll need it."

The night air is thick with heat, awful. Every breath in is stale and gross. I'm starting to think this weather will never break. We'll just choke on it and die.

Josh's house is strange and lonely looking when it's not the backdrop for the crazy parties that have made him legend around the halls of Hallowell High. The front lawn is a broad green brushstroke, and the house itself, a picture out of a magazine—tasteful, but flat. I walk the stone path to the front door and push the doorbell.

He answers in boxers and a T-shirt, his blond hair tousled.

"No," he says, taking me in. "No way. I have nothing to say to you—"

I shove my sandaled foot in the door at the exact same time he closes it, hard. I yelp and jump back, sucking in a breath through my teeth before the pain hits, and then it hits. *Fuck.* He opens the door, his mouth hanging open like a total idiot. Fuck him. I turn and hobble back down the walk.

"*Why* would you put your foot there?" he demands.

"Because I didn't want you to shut the door in my face!"

I sit on the steps leading to the driveway and rub my foot, tears in my eyes. Josh walks over and stares me down, looking every inch the asshole that he's turned out to be. The saddest part is, it's not even that much of a surprise. Josh is stupid-smart. Knowing him, he probably severed all emotional ties to me when I stopped being his girlfriend and started being a social liability.

"Are you okay?" he asks, like it's the last thing he wants to ask.

"I'm *fine*."

"Okay, good. Now get off my property."

I stare at him. "Are you *kidding* me? You're not even going to hear me out?"

His cell vibrates in his pocket. He takes it out, glances at the screen, and sighs. "Lynn Parks wants Adderall for resale because the other girls are too scared to buy from me, even though it'd be cheaper." He shakes his head. "I could get these retards Percocet and they just want Adderall."

That is not the thing he should be saying.

"Fuck you, Josh." I get to my feet. "You totally—"

He shoves his cell back in his pocket. "Okay, okay. Regina, just—wait. I'll hear you out, Jesus. What, did you think I'd be *happy* to see you after you fucked Donnie?"

*I didn't sleep with him.* The words are stopped by a dead-sick feeling in the middle of my chest. *I didn't sleep with him, he tried to rape me.* I open my mouth and close it again, while Josh stares at me expectantly, waiting for me to speak.

But I can't.

In the washroom with Anna, it made sense to just blurt it out; I didn't have a lot of time. But Josh is, like . . . not Anna. I need to think of a way to say it that doesn't betray the feel of Donnie on me.

"He tried to . . . Donnie tried to . . ."

My tongue gets too thick to talk around. A tear slides down my cheek. I wipe it away. I don't want to cry in front of Josh.

"Tears? Come on."

I recoil. "I can't believe what a total dick you're being. You're going to feel so stupid when I tell you what really happened—"

"Then hurry up and tell me, because I haven't got all night—" A car goes by, interrupting him. He *lets* it interrupt him. That's how little this means to him. And then his cell goes off again and he checks it. "It's Anna."

"Don't answer," I say. "Josh, don't answer—"

"Just wait a second. I have to take this and then we'll—"

I storm down the driveway. He calls after me once, and that's it. By the time I've hit the street, I can hear the faint strains of his conversation with Anna.

I jog down the street, trying to outrun the feeling building inside my stomach, until I can't, and then I pick up antacids at Ford's Convenience Store. They're in the fourth aisle down and seventeen steps in. I make the switch from Generic Brand J to Generic Brand K, super-strength, because I don't think the old ones are really working anymore.

They all stop working after a while.

"Come on, Anna—just talk to me, *please*."

I stretch, touching my toes. It's gym. It's too hot out to instruct, so Nelson tells us to do what we want. All the boys are playing basketball on one side of the room, and the girls are on gym mats, occasionally offering the illusion of movement, because we're smarter than the boys. I'm trying to block out the voice behind me. It's uncomfortably close and it belongs to Donnie. He's squatting next to Anna's mat and begging for her time, to get her to hear him out. She's enjoying it, but she's not about to give him anything. It's all in her voice when she says, "Go to hell, Donnie."

Kara giggles beside her. Before he made his way over, they spent the period whispering the words *slut*, *whore*, and *bitch* in my direction. Anna has also decided to torment me with fashion sameness. Today they're all wearing blue. I'm wearing green.

I felt stupid passing them in the hall.

Donnie lowers his voice. "We need to talk—"

"*Don't* touch me."

She says it loud enough that it carries across the gym, and I can't help it. I turn and look. Donnie has his arm on her shoulder, a tight grip. I can see his fingers digging into her shirt. If it hurts, it's not on Anna's face. She's cool, disinterested. All eyes are on the two of them. She doesn't waver, but he's already shrinking. His face turns red, and his gaze shifts to me, and I edge away. I always waver. I spot Kara smirking out of the corner of my eye.

"Problem?" Nelson calls across the gym.

Anna won't speak for him. Donnie lets go of her shoulder and stands, trying to recover the moment. He straightens and walks past, pausing almost imperceptibly when he gets near me. I'm the last person in this school he can intimidate. And I hate that I'm the last person in this school he can intimidate. As soon as he's across the room, I get up and head over to the corner, stretching my hands over my head, trying to look casual, but my fingers are tingling and I can't breathe. Kara and Anna laugh. I can hear them laughing.

I inhale slowly.

When I face the gym, I spot Michael. He's sitting on the bench, hunched over, hands dangling between his legs, fresh off the court and taking a breather. His hair clings to his sweaty forehead, and he pulls the collar of his shirt up and wipes his face. Then he pauses and our eyes meet.

Josh jogs between us, momentarily obscuring our view, and when it's clear again, Michael's watching the game. I'm about to head back to my mat, but I stay back when I see Josh talking to Anna. Their heads are ducked together. Anna glances across the gym and tells him something. He nods and goes back to the game, beckoning to Michael to take center and sending Jack Olson to the side. I head to my mat and try to find the will to pretend like I'm doing something and none of this bothers me.

It takes, like, ten minutes.

"GODDAMMIT, YOU FUCKING *ASSHOLE!*"

The shout cuts through the hustle and bustle, and everyone stops what they're doing and turns their attention halfway across the gym, to where a few guys are huddled around Donnie. Ms. Nelson blows her whistle and hurries over.

Even from here, I can see the blood.

"Wow," Kara says behind me. "Nicely done."

"Thank you," Anna says. She makes her way over to the scene, Kara trailing behind her. Donnie's still screaming, clutching his nose. I wait a second and I go, too.

"Calm *down*, Henderson," Nelson says over Donnie's shouts. She tries pulling his hand away from his face, but he won't budge. "Tell me what happened."

Donnie wrenches away from her, and his hand comes down, revealing a bloody mess. His nose and the area under his right eye is swollen and angry, painful.

"You fucking elbowed me in the fucking face on fucking *purpose*, Josh!" Droplets of blood go flying everywhere. *"Fuck you!"*

*"Mouth*, Henderson!"

Donnie's hand goes back to his nose. His shoulders heave, and the parts of his face not covered in blood are a matching, apoplectic red. Everyone turns to Josh, who stands outside of it all, looking vaguely annoyed.

"Yes, Donnie, I elbowed you in the face. *On purpose.*" He says it like it's a completely preposterous idea, like people don't elbow people in the face on purpose, in the history of mankind. Ever. A few people chuckle, and he goes in for the kill: "It was an accident, man. You got in the way."

I try to let the blood that's still gushing from Donnie's nose fill me up, but then Nelson blows her whistle again and the moment is over and it's not enough. It's nowhere near enough.

And it just means I'm next.

"Brooks, escort Henderson to the nurse's office. The rest of you, back to what you were doing. There's still twenty minutes of this period left!"

We scatter back to where we're supposed to be. Josh winks at Anna.

I want to punch him in the face.

Getting to the Garbage Table is easier this time.

Anna, Kara, Marta, and Jeanette aren't around. Off-campus lunch. We liked to break out at least once a week, so they'll all be clustered around a McTable in matching outfits without me. I sit across from Michael; I've brought a drink to wash my antacid down, and he's got juice and a salad. The cafeteria noises are all around us, but they don't seem to touch the quiet settling here. I know he hates me, but I can't believe he doesn't have anything to say about what happened in gym. It's a big deal.

I watch him eat while he looks everywhere but at me. I used to be able to eat here. Ninth grade. Did it without a thought. Food, lunch. It didn't mean anything.

And then Liz happened.

"I don't know how you can stand sitting back here," I say. He doesn't respond. Still doesn't look at me. "Every day. Who wants to sit alone at lunch?"

He takes a long swig of his orange juice.

"It's not like I had a choice," he says.

"It's not like you didn't want it."

"I'm not afraid to be alone like you are."

He thinks he insulted me, like I should be above codependence in this wilderness, but here's how it is: Lunch with Michael is the new thing I'll cling to, the only thing keeping me from getting totally eaten alive. Before that, Anna kept me safe from people like him. My life has become the art of putting things between me and the people who hate me. Yes, I'm afraid to be alone.

Who would hold that against you in high school.

He stabs a few leafy greens onto his fork and shoves them into his mouth. I take the opportunity to study him further. His hair is a little damp, and any sweaty vestiges of gym are off him. He hit the shower and he looks good. He glances up and catches me staring at him. For a second, I swear he knows what I'm thinking. I blush and look away.

This is dumb.

"So you knew my mom, huh?" he asks, and it's a relief to have him ask because it means we have to talk to each other, and that's better than him staring at me or not staring at me and chewing food and not saying anything.

I nod. "We were friends."

"You know, I have a really hard time believing that," he says, "so tell me something a friend of hers would know."

"Why is it so hard to believe?"

"Because you're so afraid to be alone. I think you'll say anything to sit with me at lunch."

I think of his mother. I try to think of something that would make him believe we were friends. I trace circles on the table with my finger and picture her face. She had light brown hair—not like him—and light blue eye—like him—and she was my doctor, but she was a person, too, and she liked . . .

"She loved Gary Larson's comic, *The Far Side*. She thought he was—" I try to remember how she put it. "—Twisted. That's how I found out about Gary Larson. Your mom. Because she really liked him."

His face darkens. He hates and loves what I just said. He loves that I said it, but he hates that I'm the one who said it. He picks at the label of his orange juice.

"Yeah, she did," he says.

Chunks of broken concrete. A hint of a car underneath. The person inside is crushed to death. The person inside is Michael's mom. Overpass collapse.

It was all over the news.

"It's not fair," I tell him. "That she died . . ."

"You wouldn't know."

He's right. I wonder what it's like having a dead parent—how he can walk around under the weight of that kind of grief. My parents are useless, but I can't imagine either of them not being here, being useless.

"She did like *The Far Side,* though, you're right." The skepticism in his voice remains. "How did you two meet?"

She liked reading. I take my cue from that: "Library."

He nods slowly, a million miles away, absorbing this. I guess I pass, because he doesn't press it or demand any more specifics. Another tense, awkward silence falls between us. Awkward for me. I wonder how many more times I'll have to sit here before the tension dissipates.

He'd probably have to forget he hates me for that to happen.

I look around the cafeteria. Josh, Henry, and Bruce are laughing obnoxiously together. Josh looks so proud of himself for what he did to Donnie.

I turn back to Michael. His Moleskine catches my eye, triggering a memory. Eager to fill the silence, I start babbling more things I know about his mom, just so I can hear him say something back. I bet if I talked about her enough he'd forget he hates me.

"She was really big on writing things down," I say. I nod at the Moleskine. "Is that why you keep that thing? She always used to say, 'Write it down today, put it away, make sense of it tomorrow.'"

"Yeah, she always used to say that to her patients," he says, nodding. *Oh my God. Oh no. Why did I say that?* It dawns on him slowly, horribly. His eyes widen and he laughs in disbelief. "You have got to be fucking kidding me."

My face turns red.

"*You?*" he asks. "*You* were one of her patients?"

"I'm sorry," I say quickly. I don't know what else to say, but I really don't want to eat lunch alone tomorrow. "Michael, I'm—"

"Were you one of her patients?"

I can't believe I fucked this up this badly and so quickly.

"Answer me."

I nod feebly.

"I knew it," he says. "I *knew* you were lying. I couldn't figure out how a bitch like you would know my mother, much less be *friends* with her."

I bite my lip and dig my fingers into my jeans and try to channel Anna so he can't see how much that one hurt.

"You were her patient. *Why?*" I shake my head. I'm not giving him anything else to throw in my face. "So when you saw my mom for whatever you saw her for, did you tell her you were spreading vicious rumors all over school about her son? Did that come up during your sessions? I'm sure she would've *loved* it."

I don't say anything.

"And then she died, and you—" He edges his chair back, like he can't stand being this close to me. "And now you're sitting across from me. . . ." He just can't believe it. "I don't know what you needed, but you didn't deserve to get it from her."

"I needed help."

He gives me a disgusted look and gets up from the table. My heart seizes. He can't leave me here. Alone.

"Where are you going?" I ask.

"I don't owe you anything," he tells me. "And forget about sitting here tomorrow. Stay away from me. I'm serious."

He stalks out of the cafeteria. I fight the heat working its way up to my face. I get up fake-casually, grateful Anna and Kara aren't around to see this, and decide to wait out the rest of lunch in history class, which is where I'm due next. I walk the mostly deserted halls to my red locker, yank the door open, and—

My books are gone.

All of them.

There's an envelope taped to the inside of the door. My name is scrawled on the front in loopy, cutesy handwriting. I rip it off and open it up. Written on stationery that's decorated with cartoon stars—Kara's stationery—is the word *pool*.

I wasn't supposed to get this until after lunch, when I'd have to scramble for my books in front of everyone.

Small mercies.

I crumple the note and make my way to the pool. At lunch, nothing happens here. It's off-limits. Two week's detention if you're caught anywhere near it unsupervised, since drowned students don't reflect so well on the administration. My only obstacle should be getting past Sadowsky's office, but he's probably enjoying a nap in the teacher's lounge about now. I push through the doors and find my books drifting across the water. I grab the skimmer and fish them out quickly. My notes are pulp. The damaged textbooks will have to be paid for and replaced.

I gather everything in my arms and get the hell out. Perfect timing; I pass Sadowsky in the halls. The books soak through the front of my shirt and trail water behind me, but all he says is, "Get to class Afton, or do you *want* another detention this week?"

Teachers never go out of their way to notice anything.

**Anna, Kara, Jeanette, and Marta spend the day stalking me in yellow.**

They're always in the background and they always disappear when I try to get a closer look. The dumb thing is, I used to do this to other girls. I know how it works. No one ever goes in for the kill, but I still can't keep my heart from trying to claw its way up my throat every time I glimpse them.

Between classes is open season. I get stared at. I get muttered insults, spewed insults, shoved, and laughed at.

I am a *bitch whore slut*.

These names attach themselves to me in the halls, flutter away during class, and reattach themselves as soon as the bell rings.

I'm between first and second period, my head ducked, clutching my books and weaving through the hall like an idiot, which is okay as long as I don't have to look anyone in the eyes. I end up crashing into Henry Carlson. He grabs me by the arm and doesn't let go. He's alone. No Josh, no Bruce, no Anna. But Anna's always here, even when she's not.

"Better watch it, Afton," he says, grinning. I jerk my arm away, and he frowns, like I've wounded him. "Ouch. What's the rush?"

"I have a class to get to." I try to step around him, and he blocks my path. I sigh and level a glare at him, like any look I give him could make him submit. "Get out of my way."

"Just give me a minute."

"Henry, I'm warning you—"

He catches sight of something behind me, and before I can turn to look, he grabs me by the shoulders and forces me back, a light push that startles me enough to send me reeling into a wall of flesh. The wall of flesh shoves me back. I drop my books, turn, and find myself face-to-face with Donnie Henderson. He grabs me by the arm and pulls me close enough to say, "You'll pay for talking."

All I can see is his wrecked face. There's nothing else. My vision blurs, like my eyes are totally rejecting him, can't handle it. I wrench away, and as soon as his hand is off me, the hall comes back into focus. People are watching.

They all think I slept with him.

They all think I wanted it.

Donnie stomps away. Henry hangs around to laugh at his handiwork, a picture of lazy triumph. I grab my books and head in the opposite direction and the bell rings, and all I can think is *next, next, next, next class.*

By lunch, I'm a mess. I spend the period in the girls' room with a bag of chips from the vending machine, but I can't eat.

I roll up my sleeves and stare at what's left of my bruises.

I want to run away and I never want to come back.

When the last bell signals freedom, I'm on edge. Spent. I get my stuff from my locker—warped history books and all—and push through a flood of students.

Totally alone.

I'm halfway down the stairs when someone pushes me from behind. I lurch forward and I'm flying, steps blurring past. I land at the bottom of them with a sick *thud.* The pain is immediate. So is the laughter. It comes in from all sides, and I stay on the floor, surrounded by it. It's amazing how one day you wake up and this is your life.

I am not going to cry.

"Way to walk, Regina."

I look up. Kara. Anna. Jeanette. Bruce. Josh. Josh averts his eyes, and Anna grins and she's gone; Kara whisks her away. They low-five. Josh and Bruce follow after them. I am *not* going to cry.

"Oh!" Ms. Arnett, the school's secretary, materializes in the middle of the crowd and hurries over to me, her face full of wrinkly concern. "That was a *nasty* fall you took, Regina! Are you okay?"

"I'm fine," I mutter. She pulls me up by the elbow and looks me over. My left knee aches, and a small patch of blood is soaking through my jeans.

"Oh, but you're bleeding. Come to the office and we'll get—"

I shrug her off me. "I said I'm *fine*."

She stares at me with her watery blue eyes.

"Well . . . ," she says, "if you're sure."

I hobble away from Arnett, everyone, and push through the front doors. The warm air envelops me, and my head is full of the fall and after the fall: the stairs, my palms pressed against the floor, Anna, Kara, Josh. *Way to walk, Regina.* Arnett. As soon as I'm out of the parking lot and onto the street, I stop. I just stop.

I think of the year stretched out before me like a tunnel, and I see myself in it, awake and running.

A car pulls up to the curb and snaps me back to life. I resume my stilted walk home. Ten steps later, I notice the car is keeping pace with me. I have this crazy thought it's Anna and Kara and they're going to egg me or something, but when I look, it's only Michael in the shoddy blue Saturn he drives to school every day. The window is rolled down, and his arm hangs out the side, casual. He taps his fingers along the door, dividing his gaze between the road and me.

"I'll give you a ride home," he says.

"No, you won't."

"Kara pushed you." I ignore him. "Are you sure you don't want a ride?"

It's tempting: It's hot and gross out, and my knee hurts. But I won't. Not after what happened in the cafeteria yesterday. I force myself to keep going, and he keeps creeping alongside me in the car. I squint up at the sun.

"Do you have air-conditioning?"

"It's one of the few things in this wreck that works."

Michael rolls up his window as I walk around to the passenger's side and get in. It's really weird to think that not that long ago, this would be Josh's car and I'd be sitting in it.

Michael pulls away from the curb. "Where do you live?"

"Keep going down this road, past the phone booth. It's the second left turn, seven houses down. You'll see it. It's the first brick house."

I run my hand over my knee. It's stopped bleeding.

"I was so sure you'd go crawling back to them by now," he comments. "I'm amazed you have any pride."

I don't say anything for a minute.

"I bet you're sure of a lot of things." I eye the Moleskine resting on the dash. "All you do is watch us and write."

"Yeah."

"So what do you see?"

"Everyone's afraid." He looks at me. "But no one more than you."

I point. "That's my house."

He eases the car to a halt and lets it idle while I sit there and try to think of something to say, but I can't. I get out of the car and step back into the heat, stand on the curb, and watch him pull out. As soon as the Saturn is a speck in the distance, I roll up the leg of my jeans and inspect the damage. Superficial wound.

It still really stings, though.

I'm in the girls' washroom when Kara comes in. She's in red.

Today they're wearing red.

She takes her place beside me, and our eyes meet in the mirrors. I rinse the lather from my hands and watch the suds swirl down the drain. I turn the water off and reach for the paper towels resting in a nearby puddle of water. Kara pushes the soap dispenser and lets the electric green liquid gush onto the cheap plastic counter below.

I just want to kill her. I've never felt a more honest urge in my life.

"You look like shit," she says. "It suits you."

"You'll pay for this," I tell her. It's an empty threat. Empty threats and the strong urge to bash her head against the pavement—the only two things I seem to have these days. They're better than nothing.

"No, I won't," Kara says. Her eyes light up. "Hey, I never said thank you, did I?"

"That's so fucked up. Do you even get what Donnie—"

"Yeah, and I should thank him, too. It's like winning the lottery. I couldn't believe you actually thought I'd *want* to help you after everything you've done to me—"

"I was *a lot* nicer to you than I could've been—"

"No," she interrupts. "You weren't."

We stare at each other. There's always this one girl. She's desperate and she's weird and she's jealous, and you're stuck with her, no matter how hard you try to get her off your back. Just throw some really fucked-up self-esteem issues into the mix and you have Kara. She could never keep up with us, and she knew it. And we knew it. And she was fat. Our relationship is as simple as it is complicated. I played messenger for Anna one too many times.

And I guess I enjoyed it more than I should have.

"The best part about all of this—" she stops for a second, unable to contain herself. "Is how *awesomely* Anna sold you out. I thought she'd hold back a little, but she told me *everything*. I never had anything on you before—nothing she'd let me get away with using—but now . . . it's going to be a great year, Regina."

"Just wait until she finds out you lied to her."

"It's not going to happen. And what are you going to do about it, anyway? It's not like you can rally the troops. You have no one. Well, except Donnie. Maybe he'll have you."

She leaves. I'm a volcano. Something inside me snaps, and next thing I know, I'm in the hall and Kara's there, meandering, and all I can think about is how much I want her to hurt.

She doesn't see me coming until it's too late. I shove her and she yelps, and I shove her again, into a row of lockers. The sound she makes as she hits them is nice—it's *so* nice—that I shove her again. She tries to shove back, but I'm too quick. Another *bang* against the locker. Her head. A crowd assembles behind us and I know they're thinking *Fight!* even if they never say it. I can feel it coming off them and me; I'm adrenaline.

I'll give them a fight.

But before I can make another move, I'm pulled back.

There are hands on me and they're pulling me back.

"Get off her, Regina! Jesus, what the *fuck* are you doing?!"

The comedown is fast, intense. It's over. I'm suddenly aware of how noisy the halls are, that people are talking loudly, and they're pointing at me.

They all look surprised.

"Crazy bitch," one of them mutters.

The hands that are on me belong to Josh. Kara's pressed up against the locker looking like I've done exactly what I just did. Her face is red and her hair is everywhere. I shove Josh away.

"Don't touch me."

"Kara—oh, my *God,* Kara, are you *okay?*"

Anna pushes through the crowd and starts fussing over Kara, who points at me, panting. Anna doesn't miss a beat and marches over, livid. Josh moves, positioning himself beside her.

"What is your *problem*, Regina?"

I glare past the edges of Anna's red hair, to Kara, because I'm too afraid to look at her, and then she grabs me by the chin and makes me do it. I grab her wrist, get her hand off me. Big mistake. She raises her other hand like she's going to slap me. She doesn't, but the threat is enough to make me flinch, and the whole hall goes quiet.

We stare at each other. I jerk away.

*My problem, my problem, what's my problem?*

I walk away from all of them, turning corner after corner until I end up in a deserted hallway with doors that offshoot into nowhere rooms. The fight that almost was feels like a memory already, like it didn't even happen, and I'm numb all over except for my stomach, which is just acid, so I take an antacid, even though what I really want to do is scream until I can't scream anymore.

"Regina?"

Michael. He startles me. He must have seen the whole thing.

"What?" I have to fight every part of myself to let that simple word come out of my mouth, because I really, *really* want to scream. "What do you *want*, Michael?"

He blinks, taken aback. "Jesus, just forget it."

I watch him stalk back down the hall. I stand there alone until the urge to scream disappears, and then I decide to follow after him, because he can't just tell me to forget it and walk away.

He has to know I'm trailing him, but he doesn't look back. He keeps walking until he finally forces his way through the front doors and steps outside. Leaving. He's *left*. That's a really good idea. I glance over my shoulder for teachers. None.

I step through the door, and the heat is instantly on me.

Michael's already halfway across the parking lot.

"Michael! Michael, *wait!*" He stops. By the time I reach him, I'm already sticky with sweat. "Where are you going?"

"Home," he says.

Home. I could go home, to my place. No one's there. I glance back at the school. I can actually see the heat coming off of it. And I hate the people inside.

"Can I come with you?" I beg. He looks like he's about to tell me to fuck off, but I cut him off. *"Please?"*

He turns and heads for his car. I follow him.

He lets me.

Michael lives near the outskirts of town.

It's an old house. The painted exterior is flaking away, and the front porch looks tired. The wooden fences that separate it from nicer homes on either side are in desperate need of repair. He didn't always live here. He used to live in a bungalow a few streets over, and then his mom died. I always figured it was one of those situations where he and his dad couldn't stand being where she'd been, but I don't know if that's true.

I thought it once and I've tried not to think about it since.

Michael gets out of the car. I do the same. Now that school is behind us, the whole situation feels less dire and kind of stupid, like I shouldn't have come here. I wipe my palms on my shorts, and Michael gestures for me to follow him. We bypass the front door and edge down a narrow path of dried-out yellow grass between the fence and the house that leads into the backyard.

Where there's a pool.

It's in-ground. A quietly neglected piece of paradise. A few leaves float across the surface of the water. There are two chaise lounges at the side and worn-out wicker furniture taking up space on the patio. A sliding door leads inside.

Michael pushes open the back door. "I'll be right back."

I wonder if he will be. While he's inside, I meander around the pool. I get it. It's like neutral ground. It's as close to inside as I'm getting, and that suits me fine. I entertain a visual of us in his house, on a couch, side by side or something, and it's parental-inspection-on-prom-night shades of weird.

Not that this isn't weird.

I spot a fly floating on the surface of the water, its little legs pumping madly as it fights to keep itself afloat. I know that feeling. I roll up my sleeves, cup it into my hands, and seek out the least-dead patch of grass I can find. I set it down and it stays there, stunned. It's still not moving when Michael returns with three bottles and two glasses. He sets them on the table. Coke, Jack, vodka. He faces me, and I try to ignore how much I understand what he just did. At Josh's parties, I was usually the first to start drinking and the last to stop, and it wasn't because I enjoyed the taste.

It was because I hated the people I was around.

He half turns to me. "So why'd you do it?"

"She deserved it," I say.

Michael mixes two Jack and Cokes and hands me the first. I halve the glass quickly and then I polish it off. I can't tell if he's impressed or not. He takes a generous drink from his own glass, and his expression never changes.

It makes me feel even more awkward than I already do.

"My dad keeps his liquor cabinet locked," I tell him.

He sets his glass on the table and wanders over to the edge of the pool. He rolls up his jeans and sits down, dangling his bare legs in the chlorinated water. He doesn't invite me to join him, and I feel dumb about that, too, so I pour myself a shot of vodka, knock it back, and then I just go for it. I sit next to him, cross-legged, and try not to look as tense as I feel.

"What happened to your arms?" Michael asks.

I look down. What's left of the bruises Donnie gave me are in plain sight. My stomach twists. I roll down my sleeves, until I realize the act of hiding them will inspire more questions.

"Nothing," I mutter.

"Is that why you were seeing my mom?"

I laugh. "Yeah, totally. I punch myself in the arms a lot. It's a real problem."

He doesn't say anything, and I wonder if his mom actually *did* see people who punched themselves in the arms a lot, and then I feel *really* stupid. And then I figure if I feel this stupid, I might as well go double or nothing:

"So can I sit with you at lunch on Monday?"

"No."

He gets to his feet. The way he moves is so light, easy. I'm jealous of how he walks around school with everyone thinking these horrible things about him, like it doesn't mean anything. I can barely maintain eye contact anymore.

He grabs the vodka and takes a long sip from it. When he's finished, he wipes his mouth and contemplates the bottle, and there's something so beautiful and lonely about it that I almost wish I had a camera. I shake the thought away. He sets the bottle down and returns to his spot beside me. Dips his legs back in.

"What'll you give me for it?" he asks.

I stare. "What?"

"To sit with me at lunch on Monday? What will you give me for it?"

I flip him off. He laughs. I guess I could hide in the washroom for the rest of the year, but I don't know. It'd be nice to make Anna think that I had an ally. The illusion of someone being on my side. I reach into my pocket for an antacid and shove it in my mouth.

"What do you want?" I ask him.

He shrugs. "I don't know. Maybe I should stop putting dents in my crappy reputation. It's bad enough being a waster, but it's a thousand times worse being a waster who hangs out with Regina Afton, right?"

I ignore that. "You want to know why I was seeing your mom?"

"Why else do you think I let you come here?"

"Guess. If you guess right, I'll tell you."

He leans back and stares at the sky. "I can't. I have you mostly pegged, but I just can't figure out why you of all people would *need* my mom's help."

"You have me pegged," I repeat.

He nods. "You're Anna Morrison's right hand. That's the lowest form of life on the highest part of the social ladder. There's not much to you." He straightens before I can reply. "Okay, let me try: Your dealer ex-boyfriend got you hooked on Adderall, and shrink visits were part of your recovery process."

I roll my eyes. "Wow, got it in one."

"It's probably something boring like an eating disorder."

My stomach lurches. I don't want to talk about this with him anymore. "Forget it. I'm not telling you even if it means I have to sit alone every day for the rest of the year."

"I'll walk you to your classes," he says, looking at me.

I stare at him. He's serious. He'll let me sit with him and he'll walk me to my classes if I tell him why I was seeing his mom. My fingers tingle—some kind of physical response to let me know this is a deal that's too good to pass up, and before I've even really decided to tell him, I'm telling him, just spewing it out: "I couldn't eat."

"So I was right." He sounds disappointed. "Eating disorder."

"It wasn't an eating disorder," I say. He raises an eyebrow and I flush, trying to figure out a way to explain it. "I wanted to eat and I couldn't."

Everyone thought it was an eating disorder, at first, and that's when Kara *really* started hating me. It drove her crazy every time Anna slid half her lunch to me looking all concerned. When I stopped eating, people cared.

"I went to a bunch of doctors, and they couldn't find anything physically wrong me . . . so I started seeing your mom."

"But you can eat now?"

I think of the pills in my pocket. "Mostly."

"So you just woke up one day and you couldn't eat anymore? Really?"

I nod. "Something like that."

*Liz is out.* I put my hand in the water and try to ignore that voice in my head. *Liz is out.* I remember waking up that Monday, sitting down at the table for breakfast, and ending up over the sink, puking. I thought it was nerves. I thought it would go away.

"Why?" he asks. "What was the reason?"

"That's between me and your mom," I say, but it's a lie. I never told her why I couldn't eat, even though I knew. I just fed her half-truths because she was so warm and I wanted her to like me more than I wanted her to help me. And she would've never liked me if she'd known. "So can I sit with you or not?"

"No. But thanks."

I stare at him. He stares back, a small smile at the corner of his mouth.

"You're an asshole," I tell him.

"What did you think was going to happen? I hate going to school and you're the reason why. Just think about that for a minute and then tell me if you're still shocked."

"It didn't have to be like that for you," I snap. "You think about *that.*"

"I'm so sorry that I came to Hallowell and forgot to genuflect in front of your best friend," he snaps back. "Not that it makes a difference. Liz Cooper was on her knee for Anna all the time, and it didn't do her any favors in the end, right?"

"Shut up."

"But don't you want to talk about Liz? Don't you want to talk about that time you sabotaged her homework? Broke into her locker? Trashed her things?"

I bite the inside of my cheek. "Michael, stop—"

"Started that rumor campaign about her? Hey, remember you told Duane Storey she was a total dyke when she was *really* into him?"

"Michael—"

"And I've been dying to know . . . was there actually a weekly 'Make Liz Cooper Cry' competition, or did it just turn out that way?"

"Liz was the reason I saw your mother," I snap. It catches Michael off guard. His eyes widen, just a little. "You don't have me pegged." I bite my lip. Hard. "And I *liked* Liz. I didn't get off on watching Anna torture her every fucking day. She was my—"

"Friend?" he finishes in disbelief.

Once upon a time. Once upon a time, I really, really liked Liz. Total girl-crush. Being around her was so easy. And Liz liked me too. A lot. That was the problem.

*She's pulling you away . . .*

"Okay, wait, so *you* fucked *her* up," Michael says slowly. "And *you* went to my mom because *you* couldn't eat because *you* were fucked up because *you* fucked *Liz* up?"

"Something like that, yeah," I mutter.

Somehow this new piece of information only makes him hate me more. "Always the victim, right? Liz tried to kill herself, and I'm supposed to sit here and feel sorry for *you* because you feel guilty about it?"

"She tried to kill herself?" I whisper.

"Oh, you didn't know?" He nods. "Took a bunch of pills over spring break at her grandparents'. Her grandmother found her." I shake my head slowly. "And she *still* came back to school. That's amazing, isn't it? And that whole time you were ruining my life in the morning and seeing my mom in the afternoons. . . . " I press my hand against my mouth. "What do they say, again? You reap what you sow."

I didn't know she tried to *kill herself.*

"Then this should make you feel good," I say. "Donnie Henderson? I totally didn't have sex with him, but not for lack of him trying *really* hard—" My voice breaks. "I even have the bruises to prove it."

Silence. He gets it, and for a second he almost looks sorry, sick. "Regina—"

"Tell Liz," I say, "the mean girl totally got what she deserved in the end."

This was stupid, coming here. I turn away from him, make my way across the concrete to that small strip of grass that will lead me out. I'm almost there when he calls my name, and then I stop and he says, "Nobody deserves that."

My house is quiet. Empty.

My parents work. They work and work and work. Except there's no work in Hallowell, so they go to the city, even though they're too old for the hours and commute, but that's okay with me because otherwise we might have to talk.

I sit at the kitchen table and press my face against its cold wooden surface. I stopped crying between my house and Michael's, but I could start again, so I just want to stay here and not move. I am not moving. Everything is fine, just so long as nobody moves me. But then the sun goes down and the room gets dark and I haul myself up from the table and shuffle to my room. I turn on the light and sit on the bed. *Nobody deserves that.* I imagine the words coming from Anna's mouth, Kara's, Josh's mouth, and then I do cry. One stupid tear after the other. My stomach doesn't feel so great, so I take an antacid and then I take another one. *Nobody deserves that.*

But I'm starting to wonder.

To: Regina Afton
From: The YourSpace™ Team
Subject: You have been invited to join the IH8RA group on YourSpace™!

Dear Regina,

You have been invited to join a fun new group on YourSpace™!
Click the link to sign into your YourSpace™ account and find
out who wants YOU to be a part of THEIR group!

Regards,
The YourSpace™ Staff

It's probably from some band. No one I know e-mails me anymore.

But it's fun to pretend to be wanted.

I click the link and I'm sent to a page that prompts me for my
username and password. I type them in and wait for the browser to
load.

A few seconds later, this pops up:

You've been invited to join the IH8RA group on YourSpace™. If
you would like to join this group, click ACCEPT. If you do not

want to join this group, click NO, THANKS (the group will not be notified).

My cursor hovers over *ACCEPT*. IH8RA. It's an acronym. I contemplate it, even though I could just click the link and the mystery would be solved. But that's no fun, and I'm smart enough to figure this out and—honestly—I've got nothing better to do with my time. My brain works to put the pieces together.

I H 8 R A. IH8RA. IH8RA. IH8. I H8. I hate. IH8 RA. I hate RA. RA.

Regina Afton.

I Hate Regina Afton.

**You have been invited to join the I Hate Regina Afton group on YourSpace™!**

**I throw up.**

I'm hunched over the toilet watching dinner come up, and my mind is doing this the whole time: *It might not have anything to do with you it could mean anything you haven't even seen the page yet how do you know it's about you it could be a promo for some band it might not have anything to do with you how do you know it's about you.*

Knock-knock on the bathroom door.

"Are you sick, Regina?" Mom.

Yes.

I wipe my mouth and flush the toilet.

"I'm okay. It's nothing."

"Let me know if you need anything?"

No.

"Sure."

But for a second, I think I do need her.

"Mom . . ."

She's gone.

I run the tap as cold as it will go and splash my face. The computer hums in the next room, waiting for me, and I don't have what I need to have inside me to go back in there and click the link. Courage.

But that's not going to stop me from doing it anyway.

Psychedelic-colored shapes float across the monitor's face. Screen saver. I jiggle the mouse, and the YourSpace page pops up. I stare at my choices: *ACCEPT. REJECT.* I choose neither. I click the blue link to take me to the group's page to see what it's about, because even though I know what it's about, some small part of me hopes I'm wrong.

The page loads.

I fall back into the chair. The soft sounds of the television in the living room drift in, and then other sounds follow: Dad rocking in his recliner. Mom washing dishes in the kitchen. I can hear the clinking of glass in the sink. A day off. A fan *whirs* next to me, raising warm air. It's all so quiet and so family and it's so perfect, and I have to share it with this—a page as red as my locker.

In the upper right-hand corner of it is a picture of me. I minimize the screen, horrified, before pulling it up again. It's not a nice picture. It wouldn't be. I'm staring at the camera through half lids, caught in midblink. I look stoned. My mouth is lax, and my hair is sticking out at all ends. I'm not stoned. Anna woke me with the camera at a sleepover, and twenty-four hours later she had prints. It's hideous.

The entire world can look at it, and they can see me hideous.

**THIS IS A GROUP FOR PEOPLE WHO HATE REGINA AFTON. DO YOU HATE REGINA AFTON? FRIEND US AND LEAVE A COMMENT!!**

I scroll down. The group has only one interest listed—hating me. Anna heads up the featured friends, followed by Josh—

And Kara and Marta and Jeanette and—

IH8RA has 300 friends in total. There are only 450 students at Hallowell High. The remaining 150 either don't have a YourSpace account or they haven't checked their e-mail yet. I click through the page slowly, checking out avatars, recognizing faces. So many people. Some I've spoken to, others I've never spoken to. Some I loathe, others I've never spared a second thought. A few I considered acquaintances. They're all here, all tied together by their apparent hatred of me.

I navigate back to the main page, to the comments.

**YOU ARE VIEWING THE MOST RECENT OF 202 COMMENTS.**

I shouldn't read them.
I have to read them.

**i fuckin hate that bitch.**

The first—and latest—comment belongs to Jake Martin, some sophomore I've never really given a damn about. I thought he felt the same about me, but I guess not.
I guess he fuckin hates me.

**Team Anna! :)**

Kara, Jeanette, and Marta leave this comment several times, smiley face and all.
Team Anna.

**Thnx for the add.**

My less-astute classmates leave this comment. The ones who add anyone and everything and drop a little thank-you note before moving on to the next one, because that's social networking for you. They don't get it.
Or maybe they get it and they just don't care.

**slut**
**whore**
**tramp**
**keep trying with those sweaters, regina! they can't hide what a**
   **slut u r**
**loose**
**slut**
**whore**

slut
i fuckin hate that bitch
i fuckin hate that bitch
i fuckin hate that bitch
slut
thnx for the add
Team Anna! :)

The same things over and over again. Each comment taking a cue from the last, each one a sharp jab at me. After a while, I even start feeling bruised. I scroll all the way down to the bottom of the page, and a link catches my eye:

REPORT ABUSE

My cursor hovers over it. *Click it. Click it.* Report abuse. Easy:
*Dear YourSpace, I'd like to report abuse.*
*My friends are abusing me.*

REPORT ABUSE

I refresh the page, and the friend count has jumped. 302. So have the comments. 203. I refresh again and the comments jump again. 204. I straighten. People hate me and they're online right now, hating me. I want to know who they are and I want to know what they'll say. I *have* to know, so when I step into school tomorrow I'll have every comment tied to a face, so when I see those faces in the halls—I'll know.

I refresh the page.

# monday

The buzz of my alarm clock jolts me awake. My mouth is parched and there's a crick in my neck. It takes me a minute to remember why I'm not in bed. I fell asleep in front of the computer. The last time I looked at the YourSpace page, it was 6:00 A.M.

Now it's a quarter after eight.

Forget coffee; I barely have time to get dressed, brush my teeth and hair. It isn't until I'm racing across the parking lot that I realize how stupid this is: I'm *rushing* to get to *school*. When I reach the front doors, I hit a wall. I can't step inside. I have one hand on the door handle, and it's like I'm paralyzed. My mind tells my hand to open the door, but my hand won't do it. My insides are made up of millions of feral butterflies gnawing at every bit of peace inside of me until there's none. I can't open this door.

"Fucking *move*," someone mutters behind me. When I don't, they shove me out of the way. It's "Thnx for the Add." Nora Green. She glares at me, opens the door, and steps inside. I follow her in before it swings shut in my face.

I'm ten steps in when "Slut," "Whore," and "Loose" walk by. Jeri Waters, Elliott Pike, Mary Schwartz. "I fuckin hate that bitch" is talking to Gary Doyle at Gary's locker. I start to shake. They both look me up and down when I pass.

Donnie is crossing the hall. I don't notice him until it's too late.

We slam into each other and stumble backward. He looks as bad as me, maybe worse. Unshaven, dirty, disgusting, wrecked.

*It's only been a week.*

He glares at me and then he gets close, so close his mouth is inches from mine. I'm afraid he's going to do something like he did at Josh's party, and I wonder if anyone would do anything about it if he did, because they all hate me.

"Die," he says, and then he walks away. I close my eyes, trying to keep it together, and when I open them, Michael is halfway down the hall, at the water fountain, watching me.

I head for my locker, where my lock refuses me. I try it over and over and over again and nothing happens. So I kick it.

"What's the problem?"

Michael. Behind me. I point at the lock. "I can't get it open." I swallow hard. "It won't open."

I must look really pathetic, because he nudges me aside gently and grabs the lock. I can smell his aftershave. Sort of earthy and clean at the same time. I take a step back because I don't want to be this close to him.

"What's your combination?" he asks.

"Uh . . ." *Never tell anyone your locker combination.* Ninth-grade orientation. It was the first thing they told us, but who follows the rules? "Twelve, twenty, thirty-two, and two . . ."

I watch his thumb spin the dial slowly, each number hitting its mark like I swear to God my thumb did. I rest my head against the locker.

"Maybe you should sit with me at lunch," he says after a minute. "Maybe it's safer that way. . . ."

"I didn't tell you about Donnie so you'd feel sorry for me."

"Your call." He gives the lock a jerk. It breaks free. Miracle. "There you go."

When I raise my head to thank him, he's gone.

"I told them to set up the net," Nelson mutters, surveying the gym. "Where. Is. It?"

I don't know who "they" are, but I'd hate to be them when they run into Nelson later. Red creeps up her neck to her face: She's ready to blow. I overheard someone say her name and the word *hangover* in the same sentence earlier, and I think it might be true, because she hasn't touched her whistle.

"Morrison!" she barks. "Afton! Go get the volleyball net out of the storage room, and the rest of you, get out there and jog until I tell you to stop!"

No one moves. Everyone's holding their breath. It's so quiet I can hear the vein pulsing in Nelson's forehead. *Morrison* as in Anna. *Afton* as in me. The net in storage. *Morrison! Afton! Go get the volleyball net out of storage.* Together.

"What's the matter with you people? Didn't you hear me?" Nelson winces at the sound of her own voice. "*Move!* Morrison, Afton, don't make me tell you twice!"

"Ms. Nelson," Anna whines from her spot beside Kara and Josh, "can't Kara come with me instead?"

I glance at Michael. He's across the gym standing near some guys, not quite a part of their group but definitely a part of the scene. He rolls his eyes, bored.

Muttering. The people around us are muttering. Nelson takes several deep breaths in and out, like Anna's just asked her the stupidest question in the world.

"*Morrison,*" she repeats, "and *Afton*. Get. The. Net."

She jerks her thumb at the door. Anna's not dumb enough to tempt fate twice. Josh squeezes her shoulder sympathetically. Anna gives a horsey shake of her head, turns to Kara, mutters something bitchy, and walks across the room like she's on a catwalk, leaving me to chase after her.

"The rest of you, *jog!*" Nelson shouts.

The jogging starts up—a stampede. Noise explosion. As Anna and I exit the gym, Nelson orders everyone to do sit-ups instead.

"Don't talk to me," Anna says, as we march down the hall. "I'm serious. Anything you want to say to me, I don't want to hear."

"I don't have anything to say to you."

"Good," she says.

"Good," I say.

"Fine," she says.

"Fine," I say.

"You—"

She makes an exasperated noise and keeps walking. I start stressing. And then the stress turns to laughter that tries to bubble up my throat and out of my mouth. It's not funny. If I laugh, I'm dead. But I really want to laugh.

That must mean I'm losing it.

My stomach reminds me this is no laughing matter. I find myself stopping in the middle of the hall, searching my pockets for an antacid. Anna doesn't realize I've fallen behind until I'm shoving one in my mouth and forcing it down, and then when she sees me, she rolls her eyes. I'm white hot, like with Kara in the hall, except I don't want to hurt Anna, I just want her to see what a mistake she's made. My hand autopilots back into my pocket for another antacid because I can feel my stomach boiling.

"Pathetic," she says.

I don't blame whoever bailed on Nelson: The volleyball net is wedged at the back of the storage room, unraveled behind a row of gym mats against the wall.

"Forget it," I say.

"You want to be the one to tell Nelson that?"

I sigh and we start shifting mats. They're awkward as hell. The first ten minutes pass in the sounds of us breathing and the shuffle of the mats as we move them. When my arms start to ache and cramp, I notice she's stopped, letting me do the work for both of us, waiting for me to catch on.

"Would you *help*?" I ask. She just stares. I grab the edge of a mat and get back to work. "Fuck you, Anna."

"Fuck *you*," she returns. "I thought I could trust you, but I should've known you'd stab me in the back, especially after Liz. You were never the same after that. I should've known you'd fuck me over."

I don't want to hear Liz's name come out of her mouth.

"Anna, shut the fuck up—"

"Don't tell me to shut the fuck up. He was *my* boyfriend. He was *my* boyfriend for two years, and no matter what you felt about him, whatever you think it was, he was still *my boyfriend*."

I let go of the mat. "*I didn't sleep with him!*"

"Shut up—"

"I didn't sleep with him."

"Regina—"

I'm going to keep saying it until she hears it. "I didn't sleep with Donnie, and Kara is totally setting you up. You look like a fool—"

"*Regina*—"

"Anna, he tried to—"

*"Shut up!"*

She pushes me. I hit the row of shelves behind us, and the metal edges dig into my skin, and then she's gone and I'm alone. I sit on the floor and close my eyes, and when I open them again, it's not quite three-thirty, but close, so I leave.

The air-conditioning lasts the first five minutes of homeroom before dying a spectacular death, and now I'm navigating my way to my next class through too many sweaty bodies, and I want to tell everyone to stop exhaling because they're just making it worse.

"Hey, Afton!" I only stop for a second, until I realize it's Bruce, and then I keep moving. His voice follows me down the hall. "Is it true you like it in the dark?"

I ignore him. So does everyone else. His is one voice among many.

"Because Josh says you liked it in the dark."

I face him. He's annoyingly self-assured, smug. He makes his way over to me, talking the whole time, his voice carrying over the noise, forcing people to listen.

"You know. When you have sex. You like it in the dark."

"Shut up."

An uncomfortable heat works its way up to my face from my toes. Everyone seems to have paused to listen now, and the people walking in on the moment slow down, knowing instinctively that whatever comes out of Bruce's mouth next has to be heard; that it's going to be good. A redhead and a blonde are in my periphery. They're grinning.

"Because you hate the way you look. I mean, that's what he told me." *Go to hell.* I can't say it. My voice is gone. Bruce smiles. "How'd he put it? . . . you 'wish you were a little more filled out.'" A few girls snicker behind me. "He wished that too."

"Stop—"

"And you won't let him go down on you, right? What's up with *that*?"

I force my way down the hall through the crowd that's gathered, but Bruce follows me. I try to tune him out. I can't.

"Is there something about you we should know? Should Josh get tested?"

He keeps talking. Everyone's laughing. He stays on me. I dodge into the girls' room, but he grabs the door and holds it open.

"I'm not done," he says.

I beg him with my eyes to stop. "Why are you doing this to me, Bruce? I have never done anything to you."

He doesn't say anything. He just stands there grinning. It's not like I need an answer. He's working for Anna. He's crushed on her for ages.

"Josh didn't tell me shit," he says. "Anna gave me all my lines. Is it true? Do you really like it in the dark?"

"If you think doing Anna's dirty work is going to get you a free pass into her pants, you're mistaken," I tell him. "I'm pretty sure she thinks you're too small."

His face turns red and he raises his voice. "Josh called you a *good* lay, but not a *great* one—"

I yank the door shut, but he keeps shouting through it. I lock myself in one of the stalls and bite my fist until I gag, and every muscle in my body is tight and my joints are all seized up. I breathe around my fist, sucking in air through the narrow space until Bruce finally stops and goes, and then I thaw. Slowly. The bell rings. I study the teeth marks in my skin, slimy with sweat. Phys ed. I have to show my face in front of a gym full of people who think I like it in the dark. *Is it true? Should Josh get tested?*

When I step out of the stall, Liz is in front of the mirror brushing her hair. My heart flip-flops. Liz isn't surprised to see me. She's never surprised to see me. She runs the brush through her hair, takes an elastic from around her wrist, and pulls her hair into a ponytail. I feel hollow, just like I felt in the days after it became devastatingly clear to her we weren't going to be friends again and I was going to have to make her life miserable. Enough for her . . .

. . . to want to die.

"I'm sor-ry," I say, and my voice cracks, splitting the word *sorry* in two.

She lowers her hand and turns to me slowly, setting the brush on the counter. "What did you say?"

I try to find the word again—*sorry*—but it's gone. I want to tell her she's brave, she's stupid brave for coming into school day after day knowing what is waiting for her, and I want to tell her she was the best thing in my life for one brief moment in time, and I want to tell her that I'm sorry I stood by while she was ruined, *I'm sorry, I'm sorry, I am so sorry.*

She turns back to the mirror, silent.

When Nelson orders us to stand in a line against the wall, I know what's coming next.

She'll select two captains and they'll pick teams.

Since we have an uneven class, the last one left keeps score, because the last one left always keeps score, because alternating is a pain in the ass. I've spent the first half of my life being one of the lucky ones; I've always had a team. Now my lack of a team, the lack of people *wanting* me on their team, is going to satisfy two sets of people—my ex-friends and everyone I've gotten picked over in the past. Picking teams.

How do teachers forget how horrible this is.

We line up. My hand goes for my pocket, but I stop short of getting an antacid. I don't want to give anyone the satisfaction.

"Basketball," Nelson says, blowing her whistle. "Myers and Carey, pick your teammates, and be quick about it."

Kara and Josh amble up to the front. It says something about Nelson that she never gives losers the opportunity to captain. I don't think she's ever picked Kara to captain before, and I wonder if teachers always acquiesce to these shifts in popularity, like everyone seems to, whether they really want to or not.

Josh and Kara do a sweep of the room. Their eyes linger on each of us, sizing us up for a basketball game no one will give a damn about after everyone's picked. When Josh gets to me, I feel like a piece of meat.

He nods at Bruce. "Burton."

Kara grins and points at Anna. The whole ordeal lasts only ten minutes, the deliberations taking longer and longer the less people there are to choose from, until there are only two of us left. Me and Donnie. We stand beside each other, tense.

Last call belongs to Josh.

"*Not* Regina," Anna says really loudly. I try to pretend I don't care, but I do.

It's completely humiliating.

"Whatever," Josh says, nodding at Donnie. Donnie sags with relief and makes his way to Josh's side, weaving slightly. I glance at Nelson. She notices—I can tell by the look on her face—but she doesn't say anything.

I hate this school.

As soon as Donnie is hovering on the outside of Josh's team, this is what the whole scene looks like:

TEAM 1    TEAM 2
ME

Nelson blows her whistle.

"Bench, Afton," she says. "It's your lucky day."

Someone dog-whistles and barks at me, and everyone snickers. I make my way over to the bench. The game starts. I lean my head against the wall and stare at the ceiling. One of the fluorescent lights overhead flickers, and somebody scores and somebody else scores, but no one ever asks me for the tally.

I shift my focus to Anna. Her auburn hair dances around her face, and her skin is shiny with sweat. And then I watch Kara and my fingers get that familiar itch. Instead of curbing this uncomfortable feeling with pills, I decide to stew, to let their betrayal build until I can hear the blood rushing around my head. It sounds like a dam after spring thaw. The ball goes off-court and rolls my way, and I watch Kara chase after it, laughing, and I'm *angry* and I need to do something about it.

*Do something.*

It's a small voice inside of my head. *Do something.* The ball gets closer. *Do something.* She gets closer. *Do something.*

I stick my foot out.

*Don't do that.*

But it's too late to take it back. Kara's foot slams into my ankle—it hurts—and she shrieks. Everyone stops what they're doing to watch her fly. It's one of those running falls that seems to last forever, too. She stumbles onto the floor, and the sound she makes when she finally hits it face-first goes straight to my bones in a really good way, and in the heavy pause before she starts wailing and everyone else starts buzzing . . .

I laugh.

I clamp my hand over my mouth, and her audience becomes mine. They're torn about which one to look at—her or me? Another giggle escapes through the crack in my fingers. I clamp my other hand over my mouth.

*Stop. This is bad.*

When Kara gets to her feet, furious and red-faced, she's a mirror image of me. Both of her hands are pressed against her mouth, and there are tears in her eyes.

*Don't laugh.*

The room stays quiet. Nelson jogs over to Kara, but Anna manages to get to her first. She tries to draw Kara's hands away from her mouth, and I remember Donnie, Donnie with his hands over his bloody nose and it's great, and then the tears come, tears are streaming down Kara's face and she's hurt. Kara is hurt. *I hurt her.*

"What is it, Myers?" Nelson barks. Kara jerks away, shaking her head. A sob escapes her lips, and she walks away from both of them. "Myers, get back here!"

Kara keeps her back to all of us, crying. Anna ventures over, murmurs something at her, and Kara sobs something back and moves her hands from her mouth, and I remember Donnie and the stairs flying past me and the YourSpace page and the books, and however hurt Kara is, it's not enough. I want her to hurt until there's nothing there for Anna to comfort. I dig my fingernails into my palm and breathe.

I got to hurt her *some*.

That's something.

I just wish she'd turn around and show us all how much.

And then she does.

"You did that on purpose!" It's not obvious—whatever damage I caused. I search her face and can't find it. "You tripped me! I saw you stick your foot out—*owww*—"

She covers her mouth again and cries. Nelson blows her whistle in an attempt to reclaim control of the situation and forces Kara to remove her hand.

"Mouth?" Nelson asks. Kara nods. Nelson tilts Kara's head back and inspects her mouth. I step forward for a better look. So does everyone else.

"Chipped tooth," Nelson mutters, and I finally see it.

*Chipped* is an understatement. Half of Kara's right front tooth is missing, and I wince in spite of myself, because I know how much they hurt. But I stop feeling sorry for her as soon as the picture really registers, because *she's missing half her front tooth*. That's hilarious. *Don't laugh. Don't laugh. Don't laugh.*

*Laugh later.*

"Get to the office, call your parents, see if you can get to a dentist today," Nelson says. "You'll need it, Myers."

"Ms. Nelson," Anna breaks in, "Regina tripped Kara. She was laughing—"

Kara nods frantically. "She did it on purpose—"

Her tooth interrupts her. She closes her eyes, clamps her mouth shut, and rides it out. I watch the impression of her tongue bubble up under her lip as she runs it over the place her tooth isn't any-more. Nelson turns to me, face hard. Her face is always hard.

"Is this true, Afton?"

Everyone stares at me.

"It was an accident," I say innocently. "She got in the way."

Josh's head whips up. Anna's mouth drops open. Kara looks ready to explode. Nelson orders her to the nurse's office and shouts us back to the game. There's room for me to be on the team, but no one wants me, so I go back to keeping score.

Today, it's Regina: 1, Kara: 0.

"Donnie's off the basketball team," Michael tells me at lunch.

He said it was my call, so I made it. I decided to sit with him instead of hiding in the girls' room because I didn't want to run into Liz again. I was nervous crossing the room and making my way over, but he didn't look *un*happy to see me, I guess.

"Basketball was the only thing he loved doing sober," I say.

"I overheard it in the changing rooms," Michael says. "They forced him off by threatening to tell his parents he was cheating on the drug tests. I thought of you when I heard it. I thought you'd want to know."

"Thanks." I want it to feel good, but it doesn't, because it's smaller than what Donnie did to me. So he can't play basketball. So what.

The center table is completely empty. It's like they all took the day off to go with Kara to her emergency dental appointment or something. Everyone's talking about Kara's tooth, and no one is talking about how I like it in the dark. It's so perfect I wish I'd planned it.

"They made this YourSpace hate group about me," I say.

It gets quiet—as quiet as it can get in the cafeteria—and it's unnerving. I don't know Michael well enough to understand his quiet. When Anna's quiet, she's mad or bored. Kara gets quiet when she's thinking of ways to bring everyone's attention back to her. When Jeanette gets quiet, she's spacing, and when Marta's quiet, she's sad.

"I know," he finally says. "I got an invite in my e-mail."

"Did you join?"

"No. It's stupid. They could've been more original."

Probably.

But it still stings.

Michael grabs his tray and stands. I stand.

"Thanks . . ." I say awkwardly, gesturing to the table, ". . . for this."

He nods curtly and leaves without me.

I'm sitting at my desk in my bedroom, where there's a photo of the five of us.

The Fearsome Fivesome.

Me and Anna are laughing about something, and Kara stares at us, smiling, longing to be in on it. She's there, but she never matters. Marta and Jeanette are in their own little world, forever okay with it because they have each other. I set the photo face down. Behind it is a little box. What I'm looking for.

I reach for it and fumble with the lid and find the notes.

Every year of high school is chronicled in scrap pieces of paper in this box. Our secrets. I save the ones Anna didn't get her hands on, because I knew what she wanted to keep them for—insurance, and then, if needed, ammunition. I dump the papers on my desk and run my fingers over them, all folded to perfection. I pick one, unfold it, and squint at the tiny handwriting in the margins of some old math homework.

*Are you mad at me?* My handwriting.

*Would you* quit *asking me that?* Anna.

*I'm sorry.*

I crumple the paper and toss it aside, rifle through the pile and pick another.

Another exchange between Anna and me.

*Liz is out.*

*Are you serious?*
*I'm serious. She's out.*
*Rethink this. Please.*
<u>*Liz is out.*</u>

Wait. I trace the letters with my index fingers and close my eyes. I'm sitting at my desk, writing. *Please. Please* with all of my heart. I slide the note over to Anna. She unfolds it, scribbles down those three words again and slides it back to me. And that was it. I rifle through the notes until someone else's handwriting catches my eye. It's so girly, it's Kara's, of course. I smooth out the paper and read. An old one:

*I'm at my goal weight. Now I'm readjusting the goal!*

That's all it says. No reply, nothing. It might not have even been for me. Maybe I just collected it. I separate all the papers that have glimpses of Kara's handwriting on them and push the rest aside. I examine the notes, one after the other.

*Can I hang out with you and Anna tonight?*
<u>*NO.*</u>

I don't even soften the blow. It's just there, hard lines etched into the graph paper—*NO*—underlined for effect, in case she didn't get the message, because Kara never got the message. On the other side of the page, her writing again. One question, no response:

*Please?*

I close my eyes briefly and reach for another note. I started this one:

*Quit sulking.* Me.
*I'm not.* Kara.
*Yes, you are. You have been since lunch. So Bruce called you fat—so what?*
From the earlier days.
*It was humiliating.*
*You've been fatter.*
*I look awful.*
*So do something about it.*
*Like what? Have you talked to Josh for me yet?*

I remember that next line:

*You can buy diet pills over the counter, you know. You don't even need Josh.*

*Really?*

*Yes. I'll go to Ford's and show you. I'll even buy them for you if it stops you from fucking whining.*

I stood next to her at Ford's while she bought the over-the-counter diet pills. And then, from that point on, I watched her melt. It made Anna happy.

Another:

*Are you mad at me?*

*I can't talk now.*

*Just tell me if you're mad at me.*

*Yeah, kind of.* But I wasn't. I can see it in my handwriting. I wasn't. I was just saying it because I liked gutting her. I got harder on Kara after the Liz thing. I was so angry, and she was there. She let me.

*What did I do?* Kara's handwriting. *What do I do?*

I crumple it and push the lot of them off my desk, missing one. I don't recognize the handwriting edging out into the corners of the page, and then I do.

And I don't want to look at it but I do:

*Regina,*

*I know this is a shot in the dark, but I really don't think it's that much of a shot in the dark, because we seemed to really click and I think you're cool. I don't care about being Anna's friend. Really, I don't. But I'd like to stay yours. I know she doesn't want you to talk to me, but hear me out: Can you talk to her for me? I can't figure out what I did. So if you could find out and let me know how to fix it, that'd be great. If you could put in a good word for me, that'd be even better. I really want to sort this out before it gets really bad, and I really want to stay friends with you. Let me know.*

*Liz*

I have this memory of Liz. We froze her out, sabotaged her, finished up the rumor campaign, and she had no reputation and no friends, and Anna was bored with it, uninspired, but she wasn't done, because she wanted to make sure I got the message.

So this one day, Anna got Bruce to play keep-away with Liz's books. Everyone stopped to watch. It wasn't a big deal. Nelson intervened really quickly, and the crowd dissipated, but Liz just stood there and looked so lost, like she didn't want to be there anymore. I imagine her sitting on her bed, in her bedroom with a bottle of pills.

I look at the note too long, running my fingers over the old stale dried ink.

**Josh and Anna flit by my locker. Laughing and talking.**

It's weird hearing their voices, animated, playing off each other—a scarily vibrant conversation. At first I think I'm dreaming, but I turn in time to see them walking down the hall side by side. Anna tosses her hair over her shoulder. She's flirting with him and he's flirting back. How could he resist a Siren? How could anyone? Anna doesn't like being single for lengthy periods at a time. She likes being taken and unattainable. Josh was probably in her sights as soon as he dumped me.

They're totally perfect for each other.

But in math class, I start thinking about it, and it's not okay. In ten days, I have not held his hand in the hall. He hasn't waited for me at my locker between classes. He hasn't given me a kiss on the cheek when the bell separates us. I carve myself out of all these memories and put Anna in my place, and my chest aches, not because I'm romantic or sentimental—I hate Josh—but because these were things that belonged to me and now they don't belong to me anymore.

When the bell rings, I'm cemented to my seat by this thought. The room empties, and Brenner looks up from his papers.

"Don't you have a class to be in, Afton?"

I do, but I skip it for the library. I can't wait until my parents see my report card for this term, but I wouldn't trade that moment for this one, in the library, where it's nice and quiet. I move in and out of shelves, trying to act normal, like this isn't me hiding, but it's always, always me hiding. *I really want to sort this out before it gets really bad, and I really want to stay friends with you.* This is the only reason I miss Anna: She used to tell me it was okay, no matter what.

"Don't you have a class to be in?"

That's not Brenner's voice. That's not any teacher. I turn. Michael's at the computer terminal. I hesitate before edging over. If I didn't know any better, I'd think he looked happy to see me.

"Don't *you*?" I ask.

"Free period," he says. He gestures to the computer beside him, and I sit down. He's got a game of solitaire drawn up. I don't know what to do. I watch him shift red cards onto black and black cards onto red before I turn to my monitor, sign in with my username, and connect to the Internet. I type the IH8RA URL into the address bar and watch the page load slowly on the school's crappy connection. The red background comes up first, and next, that horrible picture of me. The members and comment count have both jumped, and I think I'm sitting next to the only person in this school who hasn't joined up.

"Report abuse," Michael says, startling me.

I shake my head. He puts his hand over mine and guides my mouse to the **Report Abuse** link. The cursor hovers over the bold lettering, but I can't bring myself to click it. His index finger presses down on mine slightly, and the weight of his hand against my hand is so strange. He's waiting for me to give him the go-ahead.

"Don't," I breathe, and his hand comes off mine. He stares at me like I'm an idiot. "Anna would love it if I reported it. If I do, they'll just bring out something worse."

He nods at the screen. "Nice picture."

"Yeah, tell me about it."

"Were you stoned?"

I close the browser. "I was half asleep."

He studies me and then turns back to his game. After a few minutes, he's in total solitaire mode. It's just him and these pixelated cards on-screen and nothing else. This must be how he spends all of his free periods. He must sit in front of the computer and play games that only require one player. His face is intent. It's like I'm not here.

I turn back to the computer and then, impulsively, Google his name. The seventh result is an obituary. I click it.

HAYDEN, NATALIE JUNE
Suddenly on September 30th. Natalie Hayden
(nee Adams) of Hallowell, Connecticut,
in her 41st year . . .

It's like looking at porn. I rub the back of my neck and try not to *look* like I'm looking at porn and read through it, learning more about Michael in a few paragraphs than he'd ever tell me himself. His maternal grandparents are dead, which is something we have in common. He has no aunts or uncles. It's just him and his dad. I wonder what his dad is like. When I glean all the information I can, I x out of the page and Google the accident. The overpass collapse. It's morbidly fascinating to find the earliest reports of it—the ones with guesstimated body counts—and click forward from guesses to actual numbers to actual names. Entire families under concrete.

It's hard to think of Dr. Hayden that way. I can feel Michael next to me, really next to me, and I know I should stop before he sees me, but I can't.

"Why are you looking at that?" Michael asks. His voice is flat. I make the browser disappear, but it's too late.

"I don't know. I was just—" And then I say something really stupid: "My grandparents are dead too."

"Let's see what happens when we Google you," he says. He shuts down the game of solitaire, pulls up Google, and types in my name. The first result is some woman on a high-school-reunion site. The second is the YourSpace page. He smiles. "Funny how the last thing we want the world to see is almost the first thing to show."

"At least your future employers aren't going to think you're a slut."

I log off the computer for lack of anything better to do, and Michael does the same, and then we just sit there, staring at the blank screens.

"Do you usually do this with your free period? Come in here and play solitaire?"

"Mostly," Michael says. "Lately, I've been writing."

"That's right. I haven't seen you scribbling in the cafeteria lately."

"Well, there was this hostile alien takeover at my lunch table. . . ."

"I don't know how you can even bring your journal into this school. If I did, it'd be gone in a second."

"Nobody's interested in my secrets," he reminds me. "They're afraid of them."

"Blueprints for murder." I smile. "The next great school shooting. That's what people think of you." Pause. "Because of me."

"Because of you," he agrees.

He looks at me. The moment closes in, and I feel so bad about it that I *laugh*. It's not funny, but the tension is killing me. I stop laughing, and my whole chest is pins and needles, and I really feel like I'm going to cry or throw up, so I get up and I just leave him there, when what I really want to do is tell him I'm sorry and that I mean it, except it wouldn't mean anything to him. I don't know how it could.

"I think he's into me," Anna says, and then she raises her voice so I can hear. "Josh."

I take the bait. I look up. Postgym. Changing in the changing rooms. I'm sitting on a bench wedged in the corner, glimpsing Anna's pink push-up bra as she changes into a soft, blush-pink sweater. They're all in pink today.

Jeanette catches me staring and nudges Marta.

"Dyke," Jeanette spits in my direction. Anna yanks her shirt down quickly, like I'm sitting here and I really give a damn about her breasts. I zip up my jeans.

"I need to get him like, *alone*-alone, because we only ever talk at school, right? It doesn't matter what you say in a building full of people; what you say when you're alone, *that* matters." She straightens her sweater. "But I don't want to look desperate."

"You're chasing after my castoffs," I say. I shouldn't, but I can't resist. "I think it's already too late."

"Do you hear something?" Anna asks loudly. "Hey guys, listen to this: Did you know Donnie totally tried to rape Regina?"

They laugh. I grip the edges of the bench, riding out a wave of anger that gives me such a head rush, the room momentarily tilts. They're laughing.

They think it's funny.

Kara studies her reflection in the mirror hanging on the wall, a pink sweater clutched in one hand. Spidery, silvery lines snake up the sides of her flat, undefined stomach. Stretch marks.

"We'll do a group thing," she murmurs, and her voice sounds tinny, far away. I am glued to the bench in this rage, torn between getting up and leaving or attacking her. I can't figure out how to move and be this angry. "This weekend, we'll do some group thing and then, at some point, we'll disappear. You'll have him alone."

"Kara, you're a fucking genius," Anna says. "But I can't wait that long." She pauses. "Maybe I'll drive to his place tonight."

There's something quietly amazing about this moment, where I'm looking at Kara and she's acting like she's me. The bell rings. People filter out. Jeanette and Marta beeline for the door, but Anna holds back, waiting for Kara, who is putting on her shirt.

She turns to Anna. "Do I look okay? I look okay, right?"

Before, Anna would've rolled her eyes. *I refuse to feed into your insecurities, Kara. Own it or fuck off.* Now she says, "You look great."

"I'll be there in a second," Kara tells her. Anna leaves.

She leaves the two of us alone together.

"Get the hell out, Regina," Kara says, like the room belongs to her.

She starts fussing with her hair. She's been obsessive about her hair since the photos from sophomore year—the wig. I remember pulling her aside in the hall after they were taken. Anna told me to tell her. *Kara, do something about your . . . hair.*

She's thinking the same thing. She frowns, letting the strands of blond hair slip between her fingers. She turns to me.

"You made me hate myself." She says it in a voice like it's this epiphany she has over and over. "You know that, right?"

"I'm not sitting here and listening to how wronged you feel," I say.

"I just want you to understand what I've done to you this year is *barely* what you deserve. I'm going to make you *so sorry*—"

"But you started out too big," I interrupt. "You went too far, too soon. I can't believe you spent all that time with me and Anna and you never learned anything. I *might* have felt bad, but you pushed it, and now I'll never be sorry."

She stares at me. "Guess I'll have to try harder."

She leaves.

I don't know why, but I start thinking about Liz. And then I think about Donnie. I bring my knees up, curling into myself as much as I can on the narrow bench. I press my forehead against my jeans, and then I start to cry. I don't want to cry. Soon there's a nice wet spot on my left knee because I can't stop.

The lunch bell rings. Some girls will trickle in here to change, so they can spend the time they're meant to be eating working out in the gym. I check myself in the mirror. I look like I've been crying.

I brave-face the cafeteria, entering the bustling room and wandering through a maze of bodies, straight to the Garbage Table. Michael's already there, a tray of food beside him. He's scribbling in his Moleskine, and his face inspires another apology I'll never have the guts to give him. He stops writing when he sees me. He closes the book, sets it aside, pulls the tray of food toward him, and starts eating.

"Didn't think you were coming," he says. I dig into my pocket for an antacid. "Have you been crying?"

It's obvious. I don't know why he has to ask. "Why?"

"Just thought I'd ask on the off chance that you have been."

I stare at the table and my eyes well up. This is totally fantastic. I wipe at my eyes, which only seems to cause more tears, and when I chance a look at Michael I can tell he's trying not to look like this is a big deal or that it's weird.

"You know, you never asked me what I did to Kara to make her hate me," I say. He stays silent and waits for me to tell him. I lean forward and press my hand against my eyes and I start laughing— I don't know why—*and* crying, and I feel like a freak and I can't stop. I lean back in my chair, taking big gulps of stale cafeteria air.

Michael stares at me like I've lost my mind.

"My mom must've had a field day with you," he says.

"The second time I was in your mom's office, she asked me if I wanted a Lifesaver, and I thought she was talking about herself, you know, but it was—"

"The candy," Michael finishes. "She did that sometimes, but only to people who she thought had a sense of humor. She must've thought that about you."

"You look like her," I tell him. "She was so nice."

"She was."

"When I saw her, I really didn't want her to know I was—"

I stop. I don't want to finish that sentence, and Michael is leaning so far over the table it makes me uncomfortable. There's a heartbreaking eagerness about the way he's listening to me. It scares me. I need something to do with my hands. A distraction. I reach for his Moleskine and run my hands along the edges. It's half swollen, half scribbled in. I flip it open to the first page and glimpse his handwriting—*If found, return to Michael Hayden. 555-3409, 11 Hutt Avenue, Hallowell, Connecticut*—before he rips it from my hands.

"If I ever want you to know what's on those pages, I'll show them to you," he says, and he's flushed, like he's angry at himself for letting me hold it for even a second. "They're private."

"I guess I'll never see them, then," I say.

"You're right. You won't."

Time is going by so slow today. I watch the minute hand on the clock snail forward.

"You really didn't want her to know you were *what*?" he asks quietly.

I pull my gaze away from the clock to look at him, and he's staring at the table. He really wants to know, but I can't tell him, and as soon as that becomes apparent, he shakes his head and returns to his lunch, disappointed.

I pick at my fingernails and pretend not to notice.

It's hard to wake up. Even the promise of the weekend can't inspire me to get out of bed so I can get the day over with. The sky is overcast, gray. The weatherman says rain, but I'll believe it when I see it.

I swallow down my antacid and coffee at the breakfast table while my parents get ready to leave for work. Dad's the first out the door, but Mom hangs back.

"The school called," she says, rummaging through her purse. "I know it's senior year and you've got a lot of energy to burn, but if you keep cutting your classes, Regina, you're going to start losing privileges."

"What kind of privileges?" I ask, staring down my coffee mug.

"No more talking to Anna or any of your friends on the phone after school, no Josh on the weekends, no parties, you'll have a curfew, the works."

This is so depressing, I want to laugh. Instead, I chew on my lower lip and try to act, like, you know, wow. Never seeing my friends again. *Ouch.* I think I'll just stop cutting class, like, *immediately.*

"Okay," I say.

"Get it together," she tells me. "And have a good day. I love you."

She leaves. I wait until I hear her car pull out of the driveway and then I ease my way from the table to the sink. I fill my mug and watch as the bit of coffee I left in it turns the water murky before it goes clear. Thunder rumbles in the distance, and I stop dragging my feet. I get my stuff and step outside. It's hot, but the breeze is cool.

It's going to storm.

I've barely thought it when the sky opens up. I do that stupid caught-in-the-rain running jog for all of five seconds before giving up. I'm soaked.

I spot Michael's Saturn in the parking lot when I finally reach Hallowell High. He's in the front seat, waiting for a break in the rain, but I know that's not happening. I make my way over to the car. He rolls down the window.

"You're drenched," he says.

I pull his door open. "You will be too."

"I'm waiting for it to stop."

"Live a little."

I almost reach for his arm to pull him out of the car but think better of it. He rolls the window up, steps out, and is instantly wet. His hair is plastered to his forehead and his shirt hugs his torso, leaving an impression of the muscle underneath. A clap of thunder makes us both jump. I stare at the school. Spending the day there makes less and less sense, the more I think about it.

"We can't go in like this," I tell him.

"We're not getting into my car like this."

"Okay."

I make my exit. I don't really care if he follows me or not. Lightning flashes, momentarily breaking up the gloomy gray and sending the rain down even harder. I'm halfway across the road when I hear Michael's sneakers slapping against the wet pavement as he makes his way over to me.

It's still raining when we push through the door to Val's Diner. The place smells good. Frying-bacon-and-eggs-and-toast-with-butter good, and it's been so long since I had an actual breakfast, my mouth immediately starts watering and my stomach growls.

Today, I could eat.

"I can't believe you've lived here and you've never been *here*," I say, guiding Michael past rows of uncomfortable plastic booths. "I come here, I mean, *came* here once a month with—" *That jerk I used to date.* "Anyway, it's good."

"Checkered floors." He sounds amused.

I slide into a plastic booth near the back. Michael sits across from me. Our clothes squelch against the plastic, and water drips off my clothes, making little puddles at my feet, on my seat. The place is full of rain refugees but no one from school, which is good, because otherwise I wouldn't be able to eat no matter how tempting the smell.

We settle in and the waitress appears. Her nametag says ANGIE.

"Shouldn't the two of you be in school?" she asks, like we're the first teenagers who have ever come here when we should be there.

"No," I say, and then I launch into my order. "I'll have an egg, sunny-side up, with a side of bacon and toast and home fries and orange juice with the pulp, please."

Angie turns to Michael, frowning. He flashes a smile at her and he has a nice smile, but it leaves her totally unmoved. "I'll have the same."

"You two should be in school," she says, and then she goes.

"Food's good, but the waitstaff is self-righteous," I say when she's out of earshot. He laughs, which makes me smile. I pick at the jam packets in the glass bowl beside us. I select one of each flavor and line them up between us.

"I hate apricot," I say, pushing the pale orange packet his way.

"Not a fan of blueberry," he returns, pushing that packet my way. I alternate pushing the other three my way and his, creating an elaborate jam-packet design on the table. I can't wait until the food gets here.

"This is uncomfortable," Michael says.

I gather up all the jam packets and put them back. "I didn't mean—"

"No, not that," he says quickly. He shifts and there's this ridiculous squeak of wet clothes against the plastic. "Wet jeans don't feel that great."

"We'll dry out soon."

Michael stares out the window. It's still pouring.

"And then we'll get soaked all over again," he says.

"It's not the end of the world." I watch some poor woman get totally doused as she crosses the crosswalk. "I think it's going to break the heat."

"I'll eat to that."

We wait for Angie to bring us our food. After ten minutes or so, it comes. I zone out; I shove huge forkfuls into my mouth. Everything tastes amazing. Breakfast—what a concept. I'm halfway through my plate when I notice Michael staring. He's barely made a dent in his meal, and I feel stupid.

"I just realized I've never seen you eat before," he says.

"I can't eat at school," I say. "It's too stress—"

I stop. Awkward.

"Actually, this is the first time I've had breakfast in a while, too."

Michael looks at his plate. "Dad isn't much of a cook. Neither am I. Neither was my mom for the most part, but she made awesome eggs."

"So what do you eat? It's the most important meal of the day."

"Granola bars, cereal," he says, and then he laughs.

"What's so funny?" I ask.

"This is a very involved conversation about food." He leans back in his seat. "Yeah . . . my mom liked the idea of food better than actually making it. We were fast-foodies. It was her dirty little secret."

I shrug. "So she didn't like to cook. She wasn't making a career out of it."

"She liked to listen," Michael says. "She made a career out of *that*. And it was a brilliant one. She was really good at what she did."

"Yeah, she was." I miss her. Just like that. I feel it. I miss her.

"So—when did you hear? I mean, when did you hear about . . . it happening?" he asks.

I can't remember exactly how I heard. My parents. It was one of my parents. It wasn't that long after. I take a sip of juice, buying time, hoping he can't see it on my face. The diner's phone rings, sparking a memory.

"The office called the week it happened," I say. "We sent a card."

"We got lots of cards," Michael says, nodding. "She had this one patient, he had OCD, like, bad. He freaked when she died. He left all these messages at the office. . . ."

He trails off and it gets quiet. A month ago I would have never pictured myself here in Val's Diner with Michael. With no friends. And not feeling like it's not that bad a thing—to be here with him. With no friends.

"I was at school," he says suddenly. He runs the tines of his fork through the leftover egg yolk on the plate, drawing designs in all that sunny yellow. "I don't know if you knew that. I got sent down to Holt's office, and Dad was there. He was crying and I just didn't get it. If you knew my dad, he's really stoic, right? But he was crying and he told me, and I thought it was a joke until I saw it on the news. I didn't think of her as . . . crushed until I saw the wreckage on TV. It was bad because I—" he shrugs and sets his fork down. "I thought I'd get to see her."

"You wanted to?"

"Yeah." His voice cracks. He presses his lips together tightly, and my gaze travels down to his hands. He's clutching the edges of the table so hard his knuckles are white. I want more than anything to reach over and touch his hand, some small gesture that means it's going to be okay, because that's what I would want, if I was him. I've almost gathered the courage to do it when he takes a sharp breath in that startles me and keeps my hands at my side.

"Michael, I can't—"

"No. You can't."

I can't imagine how horrible that would be.

He swallows once, twice, three times, trying to keep it together. I want to ask him why he even brought it up if he can't talk about it yet. And then his eyes get bright: He's close to crying. I want to give him some privacy, but I can't look away. I watch him clench his jaw, just fighting with himself to keep from letting the tears spill out. His mom dead in an overpass collapse—that's a waste. That makes everything Kara and Anna are doing to me nothing. Or it should.

I don't know what to do.

"The heat's going to break," I say feebly. I already said that. And then I do something really stupid and I say it again. "The heat's going to—"

"Don't." He uncurls his fingers from their painful death grip on the table, takes a shaky breath in, and pushes his plate away. I wonder if a moment like this can be salvaged. After a long, long silence, he takes another shaky breath in and goes, "So what do your parents do?"

"They work at a call center in Colfer." It's a relief to be able to say something that doesn't sound so stupid this time. "The commute's a killer. I hardly ever see them, but they're okay."

He nods and looks out the window. The meal is over. I hail Angie, who brings us the bill. We both reach into our pockets at the same time. I hold my hand up.

"I'm paying."

"No," Michael says. "I've got it."

It becomes a race of who can get into their drenched, stiff pocket first. I win. Michael's got a whole wallet to contend with, but I deal in crumpled dollar bills. I hand them to Angie and tell her to take her tip out of the change. It's still raining, not as hard as before but steady. I get to my feet, and Michael follows me out of the diner and back into it. I stretch my hands out and feel the rain against my palm.

"Well, you've been to Val's," I say. "Now you can say you've done everything, unless you haven't done the bowling alley."

"I haven't done the bowling alley," he mutters. His shoulders are hunched and he's got his hands in his pocket. I can tell he feels bad about what happened, and I don't want him to feel bad about what happened, so I keep my voice light.

"What about the pool hall?"

"Nope."

"Arcade?"

"Not even once."

I force a smile. "So what do you do?"

"Nothing. Now ask me why."

I stop. He stops. He's rigid, tense. I get it. He's embarrassed, and everything about him is asking for a distraction. He's chosen a fight. I should give him one as a favor, but there's nothing between me and school without Michael there, and more than that, I don't want to fight him. I just want to tell him how sorry I am.

But I swallow it and it settles in my stomach with the guilt that's always there. We walk in silence after that, leaving the main street for the back roads. The rain turns to spit, and eventually we turn down Hutt Avenue, and I guess that's it. We'll end up at his place, and I don't think he'll be inviting me in.

I want him to invite me in.

I clear my throat. "Michael—"

"I don't want to talk about me," he says abruptly. He slows as we reach his place. The weather, the rain, it makes his house look emptier than it did before. Like, nothing about it looks remotely homey. But people live here. Michael lives here. That's sad.

"I'm so sorry, Michael."

He takes a step back. "What?"

The repeat is always the killer. Everything inside you goes into saying the word once, but *sorry* is the kind of word the person you say it to always wants to hear twice. "For what I did to you. I'm sorry. I just wanted you to—"

"Don't." He takes another step away from me and another, up the path. "I don't want to hear it. You're not sorry; you're guilty. That's why Liz didn't forgive you. Because you just feel sorry for yourself." My mouth drops open and he nods. "Yeah, she told me you apologized. Even she knew it. You don't deserve it."

"I knew she wouldn't forgive me."

He keeps moving away from me, digging into his pockets for his house key. "Then why did you even say it?"

"Because I meant it," I say pathetically. "But I'm not a good person and I'll never be a good person, so who cares if I meant it, right?"

"You finally get it," he says. "If you really cared, then why didn't you tell my mom what you did to Liz? Because you didn't, did you?"

I shake my head. The thunder rolls, distant, the storm moving out or coming back in. I don't know.

"And you didn't tell her about what you did to me," he says. "So what did you tell her about? How could she *possibly* have helped you if you just sat there and lied to her? You wasted her time."

"I told her about Anna."

"Coward," he spits.

My eyes fill with tears. He takes another few steps to the front door. I bet he's going to relish the weekend. There'll be no stupid, crazy, needy, antacid-popping girl hanging off him in a building full of people who didn't give him a chance because of some stupid, crazy, needy, antacid-popping girl.

"I shouldn't have apologized to you," I say.

He stops, but he doesn't come back. "No, you *should* have. A long time ago."

"Michael, I'm—"

"So do you actually think we could be friends, or do you think I'm just tolerating you, or do you think I feel sorry for you? I'm really curious, now that you've bought me breakfast and all."

"You tell me," I say.

"When I think of you, I think of a girl who is so afraid of everything, she would fuck me over in a second if it made her life easier," he says. "That's what I think."

"I won't—"

"But that's what you do, isn't it?" he demands. "You did. You did it to Liz, you did it to me—and you didn't even know me. Who does what you did to people and—"

I finally snap. "Then why did you even let me sit with you in the cafeteria that first day? Why wouldn't you tell me to fuck off if you hate me that—"

"Because I wanted to call you a bitch to your face, and I wanted to make you uncomfortable, and I wanted to see you suffer up close, that's why. God, maybe I'm as bad as—"

He stops. There's this stunned silence. *I'm as bad as you.* I want to dare him to say it. He's as bad as me, and Kara's as bad as me, and I'm as bad as Anna, who killed all the things that were good about me before they got the chance to do any good.

"I ruin lives—I get it," I say. "I don't need to be told over and over and over."

He shakes his head and walks the path to the porch, and I watch him for a minute, and then I make my way home, and it rains the whole way there.

It rains the whole weekend.

# monday

### . . . Starts off with a bang, a buzz.

Lynn Parks gets caught doing lines of something Josh sold her in the girls' room. Josh spends the morning sweating until word gets around she's not talking. Holt works fast and furiously. A new rule is implemented: Students will have to sign out of class to go to the bathroom, and if they haven't returned within ten minutes, they will be retrieved.

Which is stupid, because I could do, like, a million drugs in ten minutes.

Effective immediately, there will be no more loitering in the washrooms at lunch. No more seeking refuge there during class. The teachers will *make sure* of this. This could not have happened at a worse time, because I'm pretty sure Michael has revoked his invitation for me to sit with him at lunch and I need a place to hide. My brain is having a hard time accepting life in school without a space where I can disappear.

It comes to me—that storage room Anna and I had to get the volleyball net from. Josh and I used to meet there and have impromptu make-out sessions sometimes. I lived for him against me under that forty-watt bulb, against a background of ratty old gym mats and left-over, broken equipment. I make my way through the halls, past people heading to the cafeteria and past Brenner, who is hovering outside the boys' washroom.

Usually, the storage rooms in the school are locked, because the administration values paper and athletics equipment more than its students, but this one is always open. No one steals or would want to steal mats. I step inside and turn the light on. I'll have to use this space only when I really need it, until the memory of Lynn snorting things up her nose fades and the teachers remember how not to care.

My new hiding space secured, I wander the halls, waiting for the bell to ring, a strange nervousness in my gut. This is what being really alone feels like. I take an antacid. And another one.

"Regina?"

I hate myself because his voice gives me hope in the place in my stomach that's most anxious, and then I hate myself even more because when I turn, seeing him makes that feeling worse. Or better. I don't know.

"I was looking all over for you," Michael says, causing another desperate, hopeful twinge in my gut. "I wanted to talk to you. About last Friday."

"Okay," I say.

"I don't think we should hang around each other anymore."

He doesn't try to soften it or anything; he just says it. *I don't think we should hang around each other anymore.* Before I can even try to get a grip on it, he's saying more things I don't really want to hear.

"I wasn't fair to you. I let you sit with me at lunch and I let you do it for the wrong reasons and I should've known better—" He pauses. "—Even if you deserved it."

My mouth goes dry. "Great."

"Regina . . ."

"It's fine."

"I just think it would—"

"It's fine, Michael," I say.

"I can't . . ." He trails off. I don't even understand why he's still talking, because I said it was fine. "And you're really in it, and I just think it's bullshit. It's a waste of time."

"Okay," I say. "Thanks. I'll see you—" I laugh. "Oh, wait. I won't."

"I'm just trying to give you a reason—"

"My life is bullshit. I got that part. And I deserve it. You don't need to say anymore. I got it."

"That's not what I—"

"Kara and Anna—total bullshit. Got it. And Donnie? That was total—"

I press my fingers to my lips before I realize what I'm doing. It's like my body won't accept calling it bullshit because it wasn't. What Donnie did to me is still with me. It doesn't go away. A horrified realization crawls across Michael's face, because he didn't think that far back, which is okay, because I didn't deserve that.

But it hurts.

"Regina—" He sounds stunned, like he can't believe he has to backtrack on his awesome speech about how my life is such bullshit. "Regina, I—"

"It's fine," I repeat, stepping around him. "You don't owe me anything."

**And then Kara shoves me.**

It happens like this: I'm heading to class, I walk past her, she shoves me. My books go flying, which is the point, because then she kicks them down the hall. And there's nothing spectacular about it, even though everyone around us seems to think otherwise. I get my books—by the time I reach them, they've been trampled—and walk away without looking back, and then that little voice in my head:

*Do something.*

The bell rings. I circle the hall. I circle it again, thinking. How does Anna weigh the crimes against the punishments? "Sleeping" with Donnie is worth my total destruction, and Anna thought *I* was worth Liz's total destruction, so I look at my books and try to guess how much they're worth. They're bent, battered. And I have to factor in embarrassment, too, because it was mildly embarrassing.

I don't know how long I stand there contemplating it before I realize I'm standing directly in front of Kara's locker. I've *been* standing in front of Kara's locker.

Eleven, twenty-seven, three, ten. Her combination. I've been armed with it since that day she unexpectedly got her period and had to hole herself up in the bathroom while I got her a tampon. Eleven, twenty-seven, three, ten. My hands tremble. I grab the lock.

Eleven, twenty-seven, three, ten.

It comes undone. I open it. Kara's locker is painfully neat. The inside of the door is decorated with photos of her after she lost the weight, but none from before. There are group shots of her with Marta, Jeanette, and Anna, and jagged edges mark the places she ripped me away. My eyes drift past her books—they could go into the pool, maybe—to the personal affects lining the shelves, the things you stick in your locker to help you forget you're in school every time you open it up. I grab everything quickly. This is total suicide, and she'll know it was me. But I don't care.

It takes me three trips to get everything to the garbage two halls over.

When I'm done, I feel empty, but only for a second. Because I get it; I do. I get why Anna was my best friend. Why I couldn't be friends with Liz and why I couldn't save her and why I couldn't eat. Why Kara hates me. Why Michael can't be around me. Kara lost the weight. It didn't matter. Same school, same teachers, same classmates, same friends. No chance. In high school, you don't get to change. You only get to walk variations of the same lines everyone has already drawn for you.

So I should just make the best of it.

# tuesday

I'm not even going to bother getting out of bed today.

**Anna, Kara, and Marta are huddled behind the front doors.**

It's the first cold day since the heat broke. I stand in the parking lot, waiting for the bell to ring or Jeanette to show, whichever comes first. When they move out, I'll be able to go in. I wait and wait. My hands are numb and I'm shivering. A blue Saturn and a black convertible pull in at the same time. Anna. Kara. Marta. Michael. Donnie. The moment becomes a contest: Who do I want to avoid more?

Donnie. The others didn't have their hands on me like he did. I take a deep breath and push the door open. Maybe if I keep my gaze level and stare straight ahead, the girls won't engage.

"Regina."

I jerk my head in their direction. Anna and Kara stand shoulder-to-shoulder, Marta slightly behind them. I'm stuffing an antacid into my mouth before I can get my brain to tell my stomach to be stronger than that. Anna's mouth quirks.

"What do you want?"

*Kara* steps forward. Every time she asserts herself, it's unbelievable: I can't wrap my head around how comfortable she looks. How she can just grow into that skin when she's spent years cowering and being stupid and worthless.

"I know you were the one who fucked up my locker."

"I don't—" my voice breaks, instant giveaway. I hate this. I used to *own* her. "I don't know what you're talking about. . . ."

Kara takes two steps forward. I take two steps back. Anna oversees us, her arms crossed. She loves this. She loves every second of this.

"I know it was you," Kara says.

She takes two more steps forward, forcing me to back up. Everything about her is predatory, from the curve of her mouth to the glint in her eyes. She takes a quick step forward, and I leap back at the same time the door swings open and nails me in the back, knocking the wind out of me. I stumble forward, glimpsing Jeanette. She high-fives Kara, and the entrance congests. Donnie and Michael and a few others are trying to make it through, and they witnessed the whole thing.

There's always an audience.

The worst part is, I have to sit down. Right there. My back hurts and I can't breathe. I move to the corner like a gasping, injured dog and sit on the floor, trying really hard for air. Not getting any.

"I *know* you fucked up my locker," she repeats. "Don't think for a second we're finished."

"I never for a second thought that," I wheeze.

They clomp past me. I close my eyes and imagine myself on Tuesday, in bed, where there was this brief moment between waking up and being totally awake where my mind was completely empty and it was so peaceful.

When I open my eyes, I can breathe again and everyone is gone but Michael.

"Are you okay?" he asks.

"Get away from me, Michael."

"I'm serious. That looked really painful."

"You should be happy. You totally just got to see me suffer up close."

He pales and slinks off, and it's satisfying, but it doesn't last.

It never does.

Brenner calls me up to the board to solve some complicated equation he's spent the last ten minutes chalking out, even though I'm not wearing a skirt or a low-cut top. I don't know the answer, so I have to stand there staring blankly at numbers until he tells me to sit down again. On my way back to my desk, Kara forces her chair out, slamming it into my side.

"Oh, God." She pushes herself to her feet so the hard plastic edges dig into my skin on her way up. "I'm so . . ."

*Sorry*. She never says it, but Brenner acts like he heard it, and that's the end of it. I rub my side, biting my lower lip. Kara smirks and sits, satisfied.

I want to push her down a flight of stairs.

I actually stake out a staircase between periods so I can do it. It seems so reasonable. It seems so fair. Kara comes this way for her next class and all I have to do is trip her from the side or get her from behind, like she got me, and down she goes. I lean against the wall and wait. By the time the crowded hall thins out, I'm salivating. It looks so good in my head. I have to make it happen. I *need* to make it happen.

So of course she never comes.

The bell rings and I sit down on the stairs, a slowly deflating balloon. When the bloodlust finally fades, I feel stupid. I stay on the steps for a long time, until Liz rounds the corner. Our eyes meet. There must be no other way for her to get to where she wants to go, because she sighs and begins the trudge up. Every time I see her now, I see her suicide and it makes me want to puke. She passes me. I listen to the sound of her heels as they clack down the hall. Then they stop and clack back.

I don't know how to be around her. People have to live with things they don't want to live with all the time, but—how? After Liz, every time I ate, I tasted guilt, and I don't know why. What I did to Kara didn't make me sick. What would Dr. Hayden have told me if I'd been brave enough to tell her the truth about me, that I was just as bad as Anna? Dr. Hayden listened to my select truths and said the right things—*Anna* was the bad one—until I almost believed it wasn't me, and then I discovered antacids, like that was my problem all long, and I could eat again, and it took me the rest of the way. I never thought it would catch up with me before I graduated.

"Michael told me he told you about—" She stops. "—What I did."

I look up at her. Liz is vaguely intimidating from this angle. She looks sort of mad, nose up, even though she's staring me down.

"Yeah," I say.

"I never wanted you to know that."

"I never wanted to know that."

I lean my head against the wall and wait for her to go. She doesn't.

She crosses her arms. "Have you gotten used to it yet?"

"When did *you* get used to it?"

"What made you think I did?"

"I'm sorry we're not friends," I tell her. I don't know why.

"I'm not," she says. "I'm sorry we *were*. I never thought I'd be your claim to fame. From the boring, bitchy, popular girls to the kind that go that extra mile to make people's lives hell. After me, you guys were all set. Anna owes me, when you think about it."

"I wouldn't try cashing out, if I were you," I tell her.

She rolls her eyes and walks away.

By the end of the day, my body is all bruises and scratches. My back, the door. My side, the chair. Jeanette sits behind me in English class and jabs me in the shoulders with the sharp end of her pencil until the period is over, and I just sit there and take it.

Dodgeball.

Nelson splits the class down the middle, and the divide is such that she can't be as stupid as she looks. I think she's just as bored as the rest of us, because Kara, Anna, and Josh are on one team, and I get stuck with Bruce and Donnie and Michael.

Maximum entertainment value.

In elementary school, we had a Safe Ball. It was this soft, foamy thing that didn't hurt at all but still managed to strike fear into your heart when someone caught it and took aim. It felt so personal.

Now we've grown up and graduated to hard rubber.

I'm nervous, but in a good way. I want to move. I want to hurt them. I'm a horrible person; they're horrible people too. We might as well take each other. Anna and Kara whisper to Josh and Bruce, who hangs around until Nelson shouts us into positions, then Bruce wanders to my side of the court, glaring.

Everyone gets into place. We're using one ball today, not six. Organized chaos. Anna's team gets the ball first, and then it goes to Mehmet Erdogan, who whips the ball at Donnie, who doesn't even try to dodge it. Nelson blows her whistle. He's out. Bruce grabs the ball and gives it a hard throw in Josh's direction.

"Hey!" Josh yells.

"In it to win it," Bruce says, and there's an edge to his voice. I bet he's pissed about Josh and Anna. I glance at Josh. He frowns, retrieves the ball, and sends it Bruce's way, hard. Bruce catches it and aims for Josh.

"You guys," Anna says, amused. She knows exactly what's going on. Bruce sends the ball at Baz Jones. It hits her thigh. She shrieks and heads for the side. I'm impatient at this point. One of them has to eventually take a shot at me.

I beat Samantha Mantle to the ball and throw it at Kara before she realizes I'm aiming at her. It whaps her in the chest. She staggers back, startled, and no one can call me on it because that's the game.

But the whole room goes quiet because they know it's more than a game.

Nelson blows her whistle. "Off the court, Myers!"

Kara marches to the sidelines. It's the most exciting thing that happens for a while. I dodge the ball and watch more people get taken out. I'm disappointed when Anna takes an unexpected hit from Megan Gunter. I wanted to do that.

The numbers dwindle slowly. Michael and I stay alive by keeping close to the back of the gym. We have the edge on the other side. Josh is all over, untouchable. He's always good at weaseling away from a hit. Each time I get the ball, I make him my target, until it's so obvious, he backs into the corner of the gym because I can't throw that far.

And then the game gets a whole lot more boring.

"Come on, Josh," I call. "The game's up here."

Josh scowls but he stays in his corner.

"Don't push it," Michael says. He sounds close.

"Why do you care?" But when I turn around, he's already walking away from me. I focus on Josh and shout for him to "man up," because I need to hit something with a ball and he's all that's left.

"Shut up, Regina," Anna snaps. "Seriously."

"Aw," I say exaggeratedly, "so cute, Anna. I'm sure Josh appreciates it."

"Too much talking and not enough playing," Nelson says. "Get up the court, Carey. I don't grade you if you don't play."

Josh's face turns red. He takes a couple steps forward. The ball goes back and forth and nobody's out. Back and forth. Back and forth. Back and forth. Josh edges back to his corner. I make an exasperated noise.

"Come *on*, Josh."

"Leave him alone, Regina," Anna shouts from the side. "Ms. Nelson—"

The toss of the ball interrupts her, and then—Michael's out. Whitney Lodge gets him, and it's one of those blink-almost-missed-its, where the ball *maybe* grazed his ankle, but no one can really say for sure. But with Anna and Kara insisting "It totally hit his ankle we saw it he's out we saw it," Nelson calls it. Bruce retrieves the ball.

"I was having so much fun, too," Michael mutters, making his way off court. I head back to my corner.

And then the room explodes.

I don't see it. It happens around me. Behind me. Noise. Lots of noise. At first I think it's me because it's near me, but it's not me.

Nelson blurs past me to get to—I whirl around—to get to . . .

Michael.

I was standing here, Donnie was over there clutching his face, and there was blood. Lots of blood. Now I'm standing here and Michael's there and there's lots of blood and he's clutching his face. But where Donnie was loud, Michael is quiet.

Nelson compensates by blowing her whistle so hard it pops out of her mouth.

"BURTON—OFF COURT! PRINCIPAL'S OFFICE! NOW!"

"Ms. Nelson," he protests, "I didn't—"

She blows her whistle and he shuts his mouth. "You did that *deliberately*, Burton. Get down to the principal's office *now*."

Bruce swears under his breath, earning another blow of the whistle, and pushes through the doors so hard they hit the wall. Nelson goes to Michael, and it really hits me.

He's hurt.

I hurry over while Nelson checks him out. Once you've seen one bloody nose, you've seen them all, but this is different. It's *Michael*. It doesn't look good on him.

"Is it broken?" I ask.

Michael sniffs. "He didn't hit me that hard."

"Hayden, get to the nurse's office and clean up. Afton, escort your friend down there." Nelson turns to the rest of the gym. "What is *wrong* with you people lately? This is a gym, not a battleground!"

I follow Michael out of the gym. We walk the hall in silence. He keeps his palm pressed against his nose, switching hands every now and then, trying not to get blood on the floor. I think about what Nelson said. *Friend*. Hilarious.

"I'll just clean up in the washroom," Michael says. He sounds stuffy.

I push open a familiar blue door. "Here's one."

He stops. "No way. That's the girls' room."

"It's fine."

I push the door open and check every stall twice. The coast is clear. I ignore his protests, grab his hand, and drag him inside. I wedge the garbage can under the doorknob for added security. When I face Michael, he's hunched over the sink, gazing at his reflection in the mirror. I'm not sure why I didn't just let him take care of it himself. Maybe because being around him means not being alone.

"Are you sure it's not broken?"

He runs his hand over his nose. "I don't think so. I think he just hit it the right way. Looks worse than it is."

I grope for something to say, trying to piece together what happened while my back was turned. Bruce hit Michael with the ball. Deliberately. Michael said something. Michael had to have said something to make him do that.

"What did you say to him?"

"What?"

"Bruce. Why did he throw the ball at you?"

"He didn't. He threw it at you," Michael says. "He threw it at you as soon as your back was turned. I intercepted."

"So it's my fault," I say stupidly.

"It's totally your fault."

"I didn't mean to—"

"You did. All through gym class, you were out to kill. They were laughing at you the whole time, and you didn't even notice. It was dumb."

"That's not fair."

He points to his nose. "Neither is this."

He turns on the tap. I make my way over, and we reach for the paper towels at the same time. I push his hand away, rip off a swath, and pat the counter space between the sinks. He hesitates and then hoists himself up, and I wet the towel and hesitate before dabbing at the fresh and drying blood on his face. My hand trembles. I don't even know why I'm doing it. Maybe because I'm glad he stood between me and Bruce and I don't know how to tell him I'm glad he stood between me and Bruce.

He clears his throat. "I probably wasn't fair to you. . . ."

"Hold still." He stills. I keep dabbing at his face. I dab until he stops bleeding and there's no blood and it's all off his face. But he's on to me. He takes my wrist and lowers my hand, and I know talking will ruin this, whatever this is.

"What I said about bullshit . . . wasting time—"

"I know what you meant. Forget it."

"But what Donnie did to you wasn't bullshit. I didn't mean that." He stares up at the ceiling, quiet for a moment. "Look, I don't hang around a lot of people."

"I know." I know everything. "Because of me."

"No. Well, yeah, but what happened at the diner was weird, and that it happened with you was even weirder." He pauses. "And then you capped it off with that apology and it was—it just made me really angry."

"I didn't mean to make you angry," I say. "I'm sorry."

"I know you didn't. . . ." He clears his throat again and looks at me. "And I believe you when you say you're sorry, but it's so much easier for me to think of you as a total bitch, you have no idea."

"You *don't* think I'm a total bitch?"

I wish I could take it back as soon as it's out of my mouth. It's embarrassing. I have to look away from him. But I can't even describe what that feels like—that there was a moment where Michael didn't hate me for what I did to him.

It makes me feel human.

"Maybe," he says quietly. "But I feel like that's what I have to keep doing. . . ."

I can't hold that against him. I get how important the illusion is. If the difference between Michael thinking of me as a total bitch and not thinking of me as a total bitch is him trying his hardest not to cry at a restaurant, hurting over his dead mother—I'd think of me as a bitch, too.

"I didn't want her to know how mean I was," I say.

"What?"

"Your mom." I try to swallow and can't. "Because she was so nice and warm and funny and caring and she listened, and I just wanted her to like me, because everyone here hates me, and the people that didn't, like Anna, made me hate myself. So I . . . just wanted her to think I was good. And I didn't tell her about what I did to you or Liz because I really, really liked her and I didn't want her to hate me too."

He gets the saddest look on his face.

"Regina, she wouldn't have hated you," he says. "Even if she knew, I doubt she would've hated you. She wouldn't have been happy, but she would have helped you. . . ."

His breath catches in his throat, like he just realized it: She wouldn't have hated me and she would've helped me. And I don't know if he hates knowing that or not. He's still holding my wrist, his fingers pulsing against my skin. I stay still because I know if I move it will stop. I don't want it to stop.

What changes a moment like this.

I move forward, tentatively, and his hand stays on my wrist. It's going to be a kiss. Even if he hates it. One of those out-of-nowhere kisses. It has to be.

I want it to be.

He moves closer—

And then he stops.

We stare at each other, and I want to ask him why, but before I can gather the nerve, he slides off the counter and we're closer than ever. He exhales slowly and edges away. He moves the garbage can and leaves the washroom, and I stay there too long, my stomach all twisted up, until I'm caught by Ms. Crager, who's on washroom duty.

Strike one, she tells me.

# friday

"I'll drive you to school today."

I choke on my coffee. "What?"

"I'll drive you to school today," Mom says, and I'm all over it, protesting—*no, it's okay, forget it*—when she holds up her hand. "No arguments, Regina."

I get the kind of uneasy feeling that begs for an antacid. This cannot mean anything good. I finish my coffee, get my things, and follow Mom to her car. It's total silence as she pulls out of the driveway, and then when we hit the road she says, "We have a meeting with your principal today. It should be fun."

I close my eyes and lean my head against the seat, and the word *fuck* just repeats itself over and over in my head, because *fuck*.

"So do you want to tell me what's going on before we get there, or do I have to play twenty questions with your principal? Because I don't have the time—"

"It's nothing." I open my eyes. "It's just—"

"Cutting so many classes in such a short amount of time isn't *nothing*, Regina. Your father and I are very concerned. We don't know where you go, what you're up to—"

"Someone spray-painted the word *whore* on my locker, okay?"

"*What?!*"

She actually stops the car. Pulls over and turns it off. She stares at me, looking equal parts disbelieving and devastated.

"Someone spray-painted the word *whore* on your *locker*? *Who?* Who would do something like that to you? Why didn't you *tell* me? *When? Why didn't you tell me?*"

The last part sounds the worst. Like it really bothers her that I didn't tell her. I'm sure it does, but I feel bad enough as it is, and I need to organize my thoughts enough to lie, because I'm not interested in dealing with the truth and feeling even worse. I just need her to go into Holt's office on my side, feeling sorry enough for me to forgive me if I miss more days after this. And I'm sure I will.

"It was a few weeks ago."

She starts spluttering. I cut her off before she can start demanding answers to questions I haven't prepared answers for. "I didn't . . . tell you because it was embarrassing. I mean, who wants to tell their *mom* something like that?"

I cross my arms and try for a petulant teenage look. Like it doesn't bother me. Like being reminded of it every time I open up my stupid red locker doesn't bother me.

"Who did it?" she demands. "What did the school do?"

"I don't know. Holt had my locker repainted."

Mom sighs and rests her head against the steering wheel, and then I feel really bad. Really, really bad. I look out the window. After she's had her moment, she reaches over and squeezes my shoulder. Like a mom.

"Oh, Regina . . ."

My throat tightens. She sounds really—like she cares. I mean, I know she does, but I haven't heard that in anyone's voice in a long time.

"I just hate being there," I say.

"Well, what about your friends?" Mom asks. "Anna, Kara . . . Josh—Josh must be a help, right? You have your friends. . . ."

God.

The last thing I expect to do—cry. In the car, next to my mom. And it's the best and worst thing I could do. The best because I have her like that, and the worst because my tears have this stranglehold on me. Now that I'm crying, it's all I want to do. I want to scream and really let it out. Instead, I stare out the window with tears streaming down my face. Stop. Stop it. Get a grip, Regina.

"This isn't like . . ." Mom hesitates. "Should we be calling someone—"

"No." I take a deep breath. "I just hate being there sometimes, and sometimes I have to leave. I'm sorry."

She presses her lips together. She starts the car, and then we're back on the road, and she says, "I'm going to take some time. We'll have a day."

Like that would solve *anything*.

"Sure," I say.

I check my face in the mirror. My eyes are red and swollen. Mom parks across the road from the school. We make our way across the school parking lot, and this is as close to invincible as I get: No one's going to touch the girl who brings *her mom to school*. I get so preoccupied with how dumb I must look right now, I follow her into the front corridor, where Anna and Kara are waiting. I'm heart-stopped, frozen, and Mom's warm and smiling, asking them how the semester's been treating them.

"Look at you girls!" She has Anna by the hands, stepping back so she can get a good look. Anna grins at her, and Kara smirks at me, her eyebrow arched. "You're almost out there, huh? Graduating and heading into the real world!"

Anna laughs. "Long time no see, Mrs. A."

But it's the *way* she says it. Mom's face changes as Anna's words sink in, making her a picture of polite puzzlement. She looks at me.

"That's true. Regina, where have you been keeping your friends?"

*They're not my friends.*

"Oh, it's senior year," Anna says. "You know how it is."

"Vaguely," Mom says, laughing.

Anna and Kara laugh in unison. Pretty-girl-nightmare-robots.

"Mom, we have to see Holt," I say. A flicker of something— panic?—crosses Anna's face. "Come on, let's go."

Mom finally drops Anna's hands and gives her a parting smile. "Right. Well, I'll see you girls again sometime soon, I hope."

Anna's eyes are on me. "That'd be nice, Mrs. A."

Mom turns her back to us and heads up the stairs. Anna grabs my arm and jerks me back, digging her nails into my skin. I wince.

"You tell Holt *anything*, and you're—"

I slap her in the face with my free hand. I'm not even thinking. Pure instinct. *Slap.* And a strange thrill courses through me, because it felt *that good.* Kara gasps, and Anna drops my arm, and I watch her shocked face cycle through every shade of red there is, because *I just slapped her.*

"Regina, are you coming?"

Mom stands at the top of the stairs, waiting. She missed it. I hurry up the stairs after her, my heart in my throat. I'm dead. I am dead. All through the meeting with Holt, I run my index finger over the tingling palm of my right hand, the one that slapped her, and I try to focus, but it's impossible because I am so dead. Mom and Holt talk about me, volleying each other toward some kind of resolution or something. I don't know.

All I know is *I slapped Anna across the face.*

"How does that sound, Regina?" Holt asks, jarring me out of my thoughts. He and Mom stare at me expectantly. I have no idea what anyone just said.

"Good," I say.

They smile. Good. They stand. They shake hands. Good. The meeting is over and it was good. I lead Mom out of the office and past Arnett, who is working diligently at her desk, to the front corridor, where she gives me a long hug and a kiss on the forehead, pushes open the door, and steps outside.

Into the "real world."

The halls are empty. It's lunch.

I've been skulking around corners, hiding in shadows, trying to avoid everyone, because everyone knows I slapped Anna in the face. I'm guessing Kara let it slip, because Anna would never tell anyone that story unless it ended with her kicking my ass. So far, I haven't managed to meet up with them since it happened. That's good. If I can get through the rest of the day without that happening, that would be great.

"Are you *suicidal*?"

I jump out of my skin. The last person I expect to see—Josh. He's alone and he wants to know: Am I suicidal?

"Fuck off, Josh," I say. I remember the day he asked me out. I needed him to help me set up Liz's locker so it wouldn't open with or without the lock, because Anna told me to. That kind of says it all.

"Slapping Anna in the face? You must be," he says. "By the way, I liked that stunt you pulled in the gym the other day. Dodgeball. 'Man up, Josh.'"

I cross my arms. "I really liked it, too."

Josh shifts his book from one arm to the other. "You're just making things difficult for yourself. If you keep it up, Anna's gonna kill you."

I wonder how far he's gotten with her.

"Having fun with your new girlfriend?" I ask.

He smirks. "More than I had with you."

"Asshole."

I'm halfway down the hall when a minicrowd surges out of the cafeteria. I duck into an alcove by the water fountain. It could be Kara, Anna, Marta, Jeanette. Any of them. The crowd passes by and it's none of them, but the group of students spot me as they pass, and I hear a buzz of recognition. "That's the girl who slapped Anna Morrison in the face." I wonder if I even have a name to these people anymore.

When the coast is clear, I continue my way down the hall. More people come out of the cafeteria in little fits, and I keep ducking into corners whenever I can.

I just need to get down this fucking hallway alive. That's it.

"I take it the rumors are true."

I turn around and Michael's behind me. My gaze goes straight to his lips. *We almost kissed.* I actually have to fight those words from coming out of my mouth, and then I have to fight to keep a blush off my cheeks because I actually have to fight to keep those words from coming out of my mouth.

I don't understand what happened between us, but I really, really want to.

I nod and lean against the wall.

"Yeah," I say, and then I laugh. I didn't believe it before, but now I really, *really* don't believe it. "I slapped her, Michael, I just—did. I'm so dead."

He leans beside me. There is no trace of the bloody nose he was sporting yesterday. He's wearing a blue sweater, and it really brings out his eyes. He runs a hand through his hair, pushing the brown strands away before they fall back across his face. He looks good. This is a stupid time to notice something like that, but I'm a dying woman right now and we almost kissed so I guess it's allowed.

"Who came into school with you this morning? Was that your mom?"

"We had a meeting with Holt," I say. "I'm missing too much school."

"But are you really missing it?"

I smile weakly. "I seriously think I need to go into hiding."

"It's Friday. Maybe she'll cool off over the weekend."

"Anna doesn't cool off," I say. "What are you doing out here, anyway? Shouldn't you be in the cafeteria, writing in your Moleskine or something?"

"I heard what happened." He doesn't look at me. "I wanted to make sure you weren't—"

"Dead?" I ask. He nods. "Well, I'm not. But the day is still young. All I have to do is step down a deserted hallway alone, and I'm sure they'll jump me."

"Maybe you shouldn't walk down any deserted hallways alone, then."

Another group forces its way out of the cafeteria. Lunch must be winding up. It makes me nervous, but it's not so bad standing next to Michael. It's safe here, in the hall next to him. I close my eyes and try to enjoy that feeling while I can.

"I could walk you to your classes," he offers. I open my eyes. "And meet you outside of them when you're done . . ."

"I thought you said we shouldn't hang around each other anymore?" I say, and his expression makes it immediately clear that I shouldn't have. "Oh. You still think that."

"You helped me yesterday. . . ." he explains. "The least I can do is help you get through a day."

"Forget it. It's not like it's going to get better," I tell him. "But thanks."

He gives me this look. "Regina, just let me—"

"No."

I walk away before he can say anything else. I feel stupid. Like he'd actually want to hang around me. No. He just doesn't want to owe me anything.

The bell rings. No traces of Anna or Kara. I wish I'd known I was going to do it—slap her. I would've relished it more.

I would have hit her harder.

*Reg—*
*This is getting boring. We need to talk. If you want out of this,*
*meet me in the paper supply closet at lunch.*

*—A*

There are a lot of ways I expect Monday to go. This is not one of them.

The note is wedged in the slates of my locker. When I open it and see her handwriting, everything stops. The lunch bell rings, and the halls filter out until they're empty, and it's just me and those words and nothing else.

*This is getting boring. We need to talk.*

I don't believe it.

I want to believe it.

I unfold the note again and study her handwriting. It's definitely hers. The paper supply closet. It's not far from here.

**Kara's at the** fountain when I turn down the hall to the supply closet. She's bent over, her hair dragging around the drain while she laps up the fluorinated water with her tongue, strongly reminding me of a French poodle. I pass her and hope she won't notice me, but she does. Of course. She straightens and wipes her mouth on the back of her hand.

"You look tired," she says.

The note from Anna circumvents any desire I have to smash my fist into Kara's face while there's no one around to witness it.

"Nice tooth," I tell her. "They *almost* color-matched it."

She rolls her eyes and turns down the hall. I listen as her footsteps get farther away. I reach the supply closet, stand in front of the door, and count to ten. I need to go into this looking right. Anna can see weakness, sense it, and I need to be calm. Calm.

I grab the doorknob and step inside.

It's dark.

"Anna?"

I take two steps forward and grope for the light overhead. My fingers find the bulb when something moves behind me. Anna. I turn. Not Anna. Kara. I rush the door, my shoulder connecting with it painfully, and I grab the doorknob just as she gives it a sharp jerk toward her, and then it's closed. The lock clicks into place.

"Kara, don't—*Kara!*" She's locked me in. I pound on the door. "Kara, I swear to *God*, let me out or I'll—"

"Or you'll what?"

"*Kara.*"

"That's what I thought," she says, laughing.

Set up. Set up by her *again*. I kick the door as hard as I can, choking back a scream until I realize screaming is exactly what I should be doing.

"Somebody let me out! Is there anyone out there? *LET ME OUT!*"

Nothing. Everyone's in the cafeteria. I'll be stuck in here for at least thirty minutes before someone walks by. *If* someone walks by.

I need light.

I go back to fumbling for the chain and give it a yank. The feeble wattage sends a dull glow around the immediate area but leaves most of the room to the shadows. I wait and I wait, and when the lunch bell rings, I yell as loudly as I can, but no one comes.

No one comes, even though I can hear them all just outside the door.

I'm sitting behind shelves of poster board with my back against the wall. It's been an hour. Maybe two. Every time I hear the slightest noise, I tense, preparing to be found. It never happens. I pick at my jeans, waiting. I have to go to the bathroom. I think I'm edging up on hour three when the door finally opens. I scramble to my feet, but the ensuing grunting and scuffling sounds hold me back and keep me from revealing myself.

"Fuck off! Get the—"

"Get his cell phone."

*"Get the fuck off me!"*

"Easy. Don't make this harder than it has to be."

*"Fuck off!"*

I peer around the shelves. Bruce gives Donnie a hard shove, sending him to the floor. He eats ground and his eyes are on my feet. I don't know if he's seeing me. I can make out Josh in the doorway. Henry.

"Got his cell phone?" Bruce asks.

Josh holds it up.

"Okay, let's go."

No. Josh and Henry leave. *No.* Donnie tries to grope his way to his feet, but Bruce gives him a sharp kick in the ribs and he stays down. They don't know I'm here. They can't know I'm here. That would be too fucked up, even for us.

I stumble out from behind the shelf.

Bruce isn't surprised to see me.

"Oh, good," he says.

Oh my God. My heart sputters and dies. "Don't—Bruce—"

"Have fun, kids."

I lunge for him and trip over Donnie in the process. I sprawl across the floor, my feet all tangled up in him. He swears at me and pushes at my legs, groaning. I get to my feet and crawl to the door just as it closes. *Not this. Not this.* I press my palms against the door, trying to catch my breath—I can't breathe—while Donnie gets to his feet.

*Not this.*

Bruce, Josh, and Henry laugh themselves down the hall. I curl my fingers against the door. *His hand up my skirt. Mouth on my neck. Not happening. Not happening.*

*Not happening not happening not happening.*

"Are you ever going to turn around, Afton?"

I need to run. I need to get up. *Get up. Get up.* I grab the door-knob and pull myself to my feet. I need out.

"If you touch me, I'll scream."

"Who would hear you?"

I turn. Donnie hovers at the edge of the light. A shadow falls across his face, adding a disturbing quality to his already grim exterior. Anna must love how badly he wears being an outcast. Or maybe he just looks this bad because he's sober.

I hope.

He moves in my direction. I shudder, feel my throat hitch. *His hand up my skirt.* He was on me. Kara knew what he did to me, *she knew.* I go back to the door, pounding it with my fists until they hurt. A voice inside my head tells me to scream, *scream, scream now, scream loud, louder,* and I keep thinking *I am I'm trying I'm screaming.*

But nothing is coming out of my mouth.

His hand is on my arms. He's behind me. Close. I jerk away and

I do it too easily, which means he let me do it. He let me. He's fucking with me.

"I don't want you to touch me," I say, backing away. I put a shelf between us. His footsteps are terrible and light, and I count them getting closer.

One. Two. Three.

"You never thought I was good enough," he says. Four. Five. Five footsteps. "And you couldn't just let me have Anna. You loved to tell her I wasn't good enough for her either, all the time. Every single day."

I take five steps back, around the same shelf, past the useless locked door. I look around the room for something I can use. Paper. Poster board. I need something heavy.

Something.

"Everyone hates me because of you," he says, quickening his pace. One-two-three. I step back one-two-three. "I'm not on the basketball team because of you. I get my ass kicked and locked in closets because of you—"

I grab a stack of paper. He bursts out laughing when he sees it and takes a quick step forward and back, faking me out. I stumble back, clutching the paper, and then he lunges at me for real and I throw it. Paper blizzard. It distracts him long enough for me to get to the other side of the shelf. All I have to do is keep this shelf between us for as long as we're in here, and we can't be in here together that much longer because these things don't happen twice—where you need help and no one comes.

"Why the *fuck* would you tell Kara?" Donnie kicks at the paper. I flinch and he answers his own question. "Oh, right—it's because *you're a fucking bitch*, that's why."

He shoves his hands between the free spaces in the shelves, reaching for me.

"Stop," I beg. "Please—"

"Why?" He rounds the shelf, grinning. "What have I got to lose?"

I back into the shelf, and its hard metal edge against my spine startles me forward. It's a split-second advantage and it's all Donnie needs. He grabs at me, just missing my arms. His fingers curl around my shirt. I hear the material give, tearing at the seam, up the side. My legs give.

He bends down and breathes on my neck.

"Don't," I whisper.

"Don't," he repeats in my ear. He puts his hand on my shoulder. I cover my mouth. He slips his hand past the collar of my shirt. I choke back a sob and try to crawl away from him, but he pulls me back. Hands on me. Touching me.

I throw up.

*"Jesus,"* Donnie hisses, scrambling back. I scramble around the puddle of vomit, get myself up, and stumble toward the door. *Open. Open. Open open open.*

It opens.

Liz Cooper.

I shove past her before she can get a good look at my face. It's cold in the hall and I'm shaking and I wrap my arms around myself but I can't stop. Shaking.

"What were you two doing in there?" she demands.

"What do you think?" Donnie asks.

Liar. *Liar*. But why bother saying it. No one believed me the first time. I keep moving. Away. I can't see. I try to blink the school into focus, but I can't. I try not to panic. I don't need to see to get out of here. I press my hand against the wall and feel my way down the empty hall. I swallow air until I'm so full of it, I think I'll explode.

I'll explode and I'll be over and I'll be done and that will be okay.

I stop and try to guess where I'm supposed to be. I must have a class, but I don't know what period it is. The bell rings. I find myself elbowed and shouldered down the hall with the type of zeal only reserved for the end of the day. It's the end of the day.

Good. God.

I edge my way out of the herd, into a free space.

Right behind Kara.

Who is giggling with Jeanette.

"I'm going to kill you."

The words fall off my lips, stunned and stupid sounding, but so true. I'll kill her. At some point, I will kill her. All of this has to be leading up to a moment where I wrap my hands around her neck and squeeze.

She registers me slowly. "How did you get out?"

"You're dead."

I want it to sound strong coming out of my mouth. I want her to know it's true; she's dead. But Kara only stares and Jeanette stares and I feel like I'm going to throw up again, so I force myself back into the elbows and shoulders and hope they push me out of here, because I have to get out of here.

An arm yanks me back.

"Who the fuck let you out? Where's Henderson?"

Bruce. I jerk my arm from his grasp and shove him, but his solid frame doesn't budge. He just stares at me, amused, which makes me even angrier. Josh stands beside him, and I know I could shove *him* and he'd feel it, so I do. I press my palms into his chest and push the fuck out of my ex-boyfriend. He staggers back.

Bruce grabs me again. "What's *wrong* with you, Afton?"

"Get off me."

He grins. "Apologize."

"Get the *fuck* off me!"

I shout it loudly enough for everyone to stop what they're doing and look, but no one does anything because it's only me and— Everyone. Hates. Me. Bruce doesn't let me go. I start pushing at him, these small stupid sounds coming out of my mouth, but no words. I'm going to cry and I need to leave before that happens.

"What's going on?"

Bruce drops my hand and focuses on someone behind me. Michael. I rub my wrist and start moving away because I don't want him to see me. I don't want to see him.

"Why do you care?" Bruce asks.

Michael ignores him. "Regina, are you okay?"

I never answer. I'm already past rows and rows of orange lockers, past familiar blond curls and a flash of red, until the front doors are in sight, and I think I hear my name again but it's behind me and I am never going back.

I go home and no one's there.

I suffocate on no one being there. I can still feel Donnie's hands on me. I get vodka from my dad's liquor cabinet, because the lock doesn't mean anything if you really want it, and I want it, I want to drink until I can breathe, but it doesn't really work, so I go to Michael's house because it's after school and he should be there and I don't want to be alone.

I leave with the bottle half empty, and it's empty when I get to his place, and no one's *there* either, and I'm so wasted, I don't think I can actually walk back home. The last time I got this drunk, I was at one of Josh's parties. All of Josh's parties. The night would always end with Anna holding my hair while I puked, and I liked it because after what happened with Liz, it was the only time Anna felt like she was my best friend.

I sneak down the narrow path to the backyard. I curl up on the chaise lounge by the pool and stare up at the sky, and the sky looks so stupid from here.

"—been out here?"

This moment started without me. I can't feel my fingers. I'm static. I blink. I'm still outside, sitting upright on the chaise lounge. I don't remember sitting up. Michael's in front of me, hands on my shoulders. "Regina, how long have you been out here?"

*I don't know.* Thinking it isn't the same as saying it, though, and I don't have the energy to speak. I close my eyes and push him away. He presses his palm to my cheek, and his hand is so warm, I shiver.

"Cold," he says.

And then another voice. "Is she all right?"

Not that voice. I open my eyes. I force myself to my feet and manage three unsteady steps away from both of them before I fall off the face of the planet. Michael's there, his arm around my waist. I stare up at him. "You told her?"

"She told me she found you," he says, like that's a reason. It's not. I push away from him, but he holds fast until I push at him again. He eases me back down on the chaise. I bury my face in my hands because I don't want Liz to see me like this, even though it's already too late. I can feel her looking at me.

"I bet you love this," I mutter.

"I'm not Anna," she says.

Ouch. I can't believe how bad hearing that feels. And then I have this thought: We probably could've been friends, all three of us—like, real friends. I *hate* that thought.

"I'm sorry," I say stupidly, and then *sorry* is on a loop. I can't keep it from coming out of my mouth. "I'm sorry, Liz, I'm sorry—Michael—I'm so sorry—"

"It's okay," Michael says quickly. "Regina, it's okay—"

I laugh. It's the least funny thing in the world, but I laugh. "It's not okay. It doesn't mean anything. It'll never . . ."

My stomach twists, awful, and I cover my mouth with my hand and lean forward, and there's this horrible moment where I'm sure I'm going to puke, but it doesn't happen. But I'm really tired. I try to curl back into the chair, to sleep, but Michael pulls me forward. "Hey, no, Regina, don't do that—"

"You've got to get her inside," Liz says.

"Yeah."

He hooks my arm around his shoulder and gets me to my feet. I'm still mad at him about *her*, though, so I try to push him away again, but it doesn't work again. He guides me toward the house, and my feet struggle with straight lines. It's not a fun kind of drunk. He swears under his breath while Liz waits for us at the door.

"Why would you—?" He stops, and redirects me for the umpteenth time. I lean into him more than I want to. "Never mind. Forget I asked."

"I was alone," I say, like that's a reason.

He gives me this look I can't decode, like sad but something else. He tightens his grip on me and gets me through the door, telling me when to *step up, be careful*. We bypass his kitchen—I want to look, but only glimpse it—and head for the living room. He pours me onto the couch while Liz hovers behind.

She could've left by now. Should have.

Some small part of her *has* to love this.

"Get her some water," she tells Michael. "Get the phone, too. She's probably not going anywhere tonight. . . . Get her to leave a message on her answering machine for her parents while she can still sort of fake sober."

That's an Anna trick. We taught her that.

"Good thinking," Michael says. He leaves. He leaves the room. He leaves me in the room alone with Liz. We stare at each other. I wish I could pass out so I could wake up so this nightmare would be over. Except it's never really over.

"Your shirt's torn. A little," Liz says after a minute. "I didn't want to say anything in front of Michael. He already freaked when I told him how I found you." She pauses and she looks concerned, like she wants to know—make sure I'm okay. But then she says, "I'm not going to ask you about it."

I swallow. "You had perfect timing, Liz. . . ."

Silence.

"Good," she finally replies, and she sounds like she means it, and it makes me feel so bad. A tear manages to escape me. I wipe it away quickly.

"When will you forgive me?" I blurt out. "I got what I deserved. I know I deserve it, everything, but I need to know if you forgive—"

"Like if you suffer enough I should forgive you?" she asks, totally unimpressed. I exhale shakily and stare at her feet. "That's not how it works."

"But I really, really—"

"Look, Regina, you're *really* drunk right now," she says, which is like *Shut up.* So I shut up and we wait for Michael to come back. I take in the room. It's tidy but empty. The walls are bare and white, waiting for color. The furniture is sparse—a couch, a chair in the corner, a television. It's like they never finished moving in. Like they started unpacking and stopped halfway and threw all the half-full boxes out.

Michael comes back with the water and the phone. Liz gives him my number. I can't believe she still remembers it. He dials and holds the receiver up to my ear. I wait for the answering machine to pick up, and then I mumble something about being ". . . at Anna's for the night see you tomorrow love you bye."

I feel like such a loser.

"I'll go," Liz says because there's nothing else here for her to see. She touches Michael's shoulder. "I'll see you."

"Thanks," he says.

Liz turns to me, and for a second I think she's going to say something, but she doesn't. She leaves. After a minute, the sound of the front door closing echoes through the house. I want to die.

Michael holds up the glass of water. He kneels down and presses it into my hands, and it's not that I can't hold it; it's that I don't want to. He anticipates this, cradling the glass in his palm. He sets it on the floor and looks at me.

"Do you forgive me?" I ask. Because Liz is right: I'm really drunk right now, so this is the only time I'll get away with just asking him.

"What?" But he heard me.

"You don't," I say. "Liz doesn't forgive me and you don't—"

Before he can say anything—before I can even finish what I'm saying—I bring my hands to his face and clumsily lean forward. My lips graze his cheek, and he brings his hands to my side, to steady me or to keep me from touching him, I don't know. I bring my mouth to his lips and kiss him because . . . because his lips are nice.

And I'm starved for nice things.

He kisses me back.

"No—" He pulls away and his hand hits the water. It tips, spilling onto the carpet, and some kind of dull embarrassment plants itself in the middle of my brain so I'll feel stupid about this when I sober up. I reach for him, fumble with the buttons of his shirt, and I almost get one undone when he says that dumb word again: "No."

I bring my hands to his face again. I can touch him into this. But he grabs my hands and says, *"Regina,"* and that stops me for the last time.

And then he lets go of my hands.

"I don't feel well," I tell him.

He clears his throat. "Go to sleep. You'll feel better when you wake up."

Right.

# tuesday

**The house is quiet.**

The scene in the closet with Donnie drifts in and out of my head. I let it in and then I force it back out. Repeat.

Rays of sunlight filter in through the minute gaps in the curtain drawn over the glass door leading to the pool. I push them aside and stare at the water. It's still. It's late morning and Michael's not home or he's still sleeping. I'm not sure and I don't want to find out. I think the easiest way to pretend Monday never happened is to get as far away from it as possible.

I unlock the door and step outside. It's cold. I can't believe we were choking on heat not that long ago and now it's cold out. I make my way around the house, down that stupid little path, and end up on the front lawn and—

Michael's there, getting out of his car. He stops when he sees me, stays by the driver's side, like he's not sure how to proceed. My face gets hot. This moment where we cross paths the day after I sloppy-drunk-kiss him isn't supposed to happen.

"Hey," he says. "Hungover?"

"No."

He's impressed. "Lucky."

"Sometimes I get a break."

He stays where he is and I stay where I am. It's a weird sort of face-off. I'm not hungover, but I feel fragmented; lost. Nobody wants me.

"I was alone, right?" I finally ask, pointing back to the house. "Where's your dad? Did he . . . ?"

Michael hesitates. "He works. But he was here. He comes home through the front door, refuels in the kitchen, goes to bed, wakes up, refuels in kitchen, and leaves through the front door. He didn't even know you were here."

"I should go."

"Wait—don't," he says, and then he turns red. "I mean, I want to show you something."

I'm in the passenger side of Michael's car, watching Hallowell fly past, a picture of midmorning quiet. It's overcast and cold, and the sun barely kisses the houses lining the streets. After a while, Hallowell disappears and we pull onto a dirt road that leads out of town. I watch as the wheels kick up dust in the rearview.

Michael is a quiet comfort beside me. I like him beside me. After thirty minutes or so, the road goes smooth and then rough again. Another dirt road. We stay on this one a long time, until a familiar black convertible comes into view.

My chest tightens and my hand goes for the door.

"It's okay," Michael says quickly. "Regina, he's not here."

I stare at the convertible parked on the side of the road. Donnie's not here. It sinks in slowly. What that means. Donnie's not here. But his car is.

And then I feel like I've chased a bunch of speed with twenty cups of coffee.

Michael eases the Saturn to a stop behind the convertible.

"He'll never find it out here." He pulls a different set of keys from his pockets. I recognize the little Swiss Army knife keychain. "Left them in the ignition. Idiot." He tosses them from hand to hand. "No one's going to give him a ride anywhere. He'll have to hoof it for who knows how long. So I was thinking we put the top down, because it's supposed to rain all week, and leave the keys inside for anyone to find. . . ."

Michael hands me the keys. I close my fingers around them. They're warm from his grasp and now they're in mine. Donnie loves that convertible.

It's the only thing he has.

I get out of the car and approach it carefully, slowly. I don't even know where to start, so I get into the driver's side, where Donnie sits every day, and think. And then I put the top down and shove the keys in the ignition. I feel empty. It's not enough.

And then I get an idea.

The coffee-and-speed feeling comes back more intensely than before. I grab the keys again. This is perfect. I get out of the car. So perfect. I fingernail the knife out of the cover. I'm vaguely aware of Michael watching as I drag the tip of the knife down the driver's side of the convertible. I press in hard. It's a beautiful sound.

It's a beautiful scratch.

And then I do it again.

Again. Again.

I step back and admire my handiwork. Four perfect scratches down the length of his classic convertible, but it *still* isn't enough. I could do better.

I need to stop looking at it like a car and more like a canvas.

I drop to my knees. My fingers are wrapped so tightly around the keys they hurt, but it's a good hurt. I move to the farthest side of the car and start making art—a big letter **D**. I follow it with an **O**. **U**. I carve deep, going over the letters as hard as I can. **C**. **H**. **E**. It takes a while. My fingers go numb. I stop at the *E* and uncurl my fingers. I rub them and wait for the feeling to return. That takes a while, too.

"Nice," Michael says, coming up behind me.

"I'm not done," I say, and then I get to work on the **B**. The letters cross over the original lines I made and this is definitely art. This feels good. I imagine the car is Kara and I imagine the car is Anna. I imagine the metal as their skin, and it feels even better. That's sick. Even I know how sick that is.

It's as sick as locking me in a closet with the guy who tried to rape me.

I drop the knife.

For a minute, all I see is us. Me and Anna. Kara and Jeanette and Mara. No Josh, no Donnie, no Michael. Nothing is complicated. We are the sweet side of thirteen, traipsing down the main street, and we're eating out for lunch, the first time off campus. It's a Big Deal. We have to get permission slips and everything. I see Marta and Jeanette, and they're oblivious, happy. Kara is overweight, dour even when she smiles, and we're not close but we're not there—here—yet. And Anna is this carefree vision that makes my heart ache, because I don't know what happened to her, but she used to be good.

We're sick. We're sick. We're sick girls.

Michael kneels down beside me. "A," he says.

I get back to work: **A**.

**G**.

Done. I'm drenched in sweat and my bangs are stuck to my forehead. I take a deep breath and press my hands against the ground and just ride it out, and when I'm sure I'm not going to cry, I lean back and stare at the car, and I can feel how close Michael is beside me.

"You did this for me," I say slowly. "But we're not friends."

"Regina," he says, "I . . ."

But he never finishes.

I stare at the ground and all I can think about is Michael's mouth against my mouth and Donnie's keys in my hands and how funny they felt against my palm, like a metal revelation.

It's like the evolution of anger. It doesn't have to be loud all the time.

Now it's just quiet and it's all of me.

I cross the school parking lot and feel like a junkie looking for a fix, but I'm not sure what my next fix is. I just know it's in this building. I pull the front doors open and step into three-quarters of my old crowd. Anna, Kara, and Jeanette stare at me like they can't believe I've done it, and now that I've done it, I can't believe it either. And then I just stand there, paralyzed. I can't move. Something is going to happen.

I'm just not sure what.

"Jesus Christ, Regina, just *go*."

I study each and every one of them, committing their faces to memory. I know what they look like, but I want to make sure I remember them this way, post–locking me in a closet with Donnie. My fingers curl in on themselves, and I bite my tongue so hard, I taste blood. *I hate these girls I hate these girls I hate these girls.*

"Are you fucking deaf?" Kara.

"Forget it," Anna says impatiently. "Marta can find us at my locker."

She moves out and Jeanette follows after her, but Kara stays behind to smirk. All I'd have to do is reach out and choke, she's that close. It'd be so easy and it would feel *so good.* But I can't move.

"*Kara.*" Anna. Her *Here, girl,* voice. I remember that voice.

Kara gives me one last look and hurries after Anna. She's fucked if she thinks I'm done with her. I take a sharp breath in, and my body comes back to me; I can move, but now I have to wait. I lean against the wall and watch people filter in until the bell rings. When it finally does, I head up the stairs and down the hall to her locker, and she's there.

Alone.

She doesn't see me coming until I'm shoving her against the locker. She makes a startled noise, but she rallies quickly and shoves me back, and I shove her again and it's my palms on her shoulders. This beautiful adrenaline rush. I will kill her.

She sees it in me and manages to slip away before I can do it.

I'm not going to chase her. Not yet.

The hall is empty. Class noises ghost in. I lean against Kara's locker and come down, but I don't want to come down. Someone shuffles my way. I turn. Donnie. He looks like shit. There are bags under his eyes and his hair is greasy. It's weird that we're living in two separate but similar hells. That Anna has found a way to make him miserable and I'm not a part of it.

I really would have liked to have been a part of it.

"Where's your car?" I ask.

He stops and looks at me, confused. Not confused about *what* I've asked him, but *that* I've asked him and that I'm not scared. I like the way it feels.

"None of your fucking business," he mutters. And then, "It's getting work done."

"No it's not."

I steel myself. I watch him process it, watch the color of his face start building to a good red.

"What did you do to my car?" he growls.

"Don't worry, Donnie," I say. "It'll turn up. Eventually."

He comes close, so close. At-the-party close. My heart beats crazy in my chest, but I know none of it is on my face, so I just keep going. "What? It still runs."

He brings his fist up and slams his knuckles into the metal beside my head.

"Tell me where it is or you're *dead*, Afton."

He's breathing heavily. He wants to hurt me, but I'm not entirely convinced that he will. We stare at each other, our eyes locked, and I raise my chin.

*Do something.*

"What's going on?" We turn, startled by this new voice. Brenner stands in the middle of the hall, his arms crossed. Donnie backs off. "Get to class, both of you."

Donnie goes one way and I go the other. *That was stupid. That was stupid. That was stupid. That was really, really stupid.* But I'd do it again in a second, just to have that moment that felt like it was mine.

I walk down the hall. All I can think about is what's next, the next moment that's mine. I'm not going to class. I'm not going to find it in class. I wander the halls seeking it out until the adrenaline fades, and the bell rings again.

It's strange walking with these bodies, all on their way to class. This is their day-to-day. Nothing bothers them, and the things that might bother them are nothing. I roll my shoulders, I flex my fingers. There's something inside me that needs somewhere to go. I feel quiet-reckless-crazy. I feel like . . . I could shove my knuckles into metal and it would never hurt. I feel dead inside.

I round the corner and spot Michael at the end of the hall talking to Liz. I stop. My heart stops. I duck into the spaces between rows of lockers because I'm avoiding him. After the closet with Donnie, the kiss, the car, I see him and I can't breathe. I'm scared of what I felt both times—when my mouth was on his mouth and after he put his hands on my wrists and told me *no.*

I peek around the corner and watch him talk to Liz. I want to see what that looks like—if there's something there when he talks to her that isn't there when he talks to me. It's effortless. They aren't into each other like that, but he's leaning against the locker and she's close the way friends are close. She says something to him and he says something back and smiles and laughs. I'm struck by how amazing it is and how sad that makes me, because I've never seen that. He's not like that around me. The way his mouth quirks and lights up his eyes. He should smile more often. It's so innocent.

I lean back against the wall and chew on my lips, swallowing hard. It hurts being on the outside of something so honest. I want it, but I don't know how I can have it when I'm so angry, and I feel so far from finished.

I spend lunch in my storage room.

I'm sitting on the floor, picking at my fingernails, waiting for the bell to ring. Legs crossed at the ankle. This is boring, but it's okay because nothing is happening, and I'm trying not to think too much, because I think too much and I never think good things. I count the number of mats wedged at the back of the room (four). I find various pieces of broken equipment in a cobwebby cardboard box wedged in the corner and organize them into piles and then put them back.

When the bell rings, I press my ear against the door and wait until all the footsteps fade away, and then I sneak out and drift down the hall.

"Hey, Regina—"

I stiffen. That's Michael's voice. He's somewhere behind me. I duck my shoulders and quicken my pace. He'll get the message; he's not stupid.

"Regina—"

His voice gets lost to hall noises, and I relax because that has to mean he's fallen behind. I don't know what he could possibly want with me. We've come to a natural end. There can't be much left after you steal a car for someone and then stand around and watch while they decimate the paint job.

I slam shoulders with some freshman and slip around them,

narrowly missing someone else. The hall is congested. I push past a few more stationary bodies because my locker's here, and then I . . .

. . . feel it in my bones before my brain processes it.

Everything goes cold.

My red locker door is hanging open, guts splayed out for the whole world to see. The hall is congested because people are pausing so they can point at it and laugh. They make ridiculous faces as they go. I edge wordlessly through the crowd so I can get a good look at what they've done to my locker this time *this time this time again.*

Rancid, raw ground meat. All over everything. My books. My coat. Book bag. The sides of my locker. Everywhere. Everything is ruined. They must have raided the grocery store and bought up all the bargain meat and left it outside for days and days, because the smell is unbelievable. Acrid, sour.

I reach in. My fingers brush over slimy bits of some dead animal.

My heartbeat slows to nothing and then, when I'm sure I'm dead, it thumps once. Twice. Three times. Steady and even. I'm still here. I get to ten beats and then it beats faster—twenty, faster, thirty, faster, forty. Do something do something *do something.*

I slam the door so hard it recoils back.

The crowd murmurs.

"Regina—"

Michael's voice sounds like it's far away, but it's closer than I want it to be. I storm down the hall, away from it. He calls me once more. Part of me wants to detach myself from this anger and go to him, but that part of me is very small. I head for the second floor. Kara's locker. She might be there. Because it was her. Maybe it was Anna's idea, but Kara would've done it.

Anna would never touch that stuff.

I crash into some moron who's decided to go down the up stairs. Books fly. I grab the railing and push myself forward until I hear this: "Thanks a lot, bitch."

And even though she hasn't spoken to me in ages, I haven't forgotten that blonde's breathy voice yet. Jeanette bends down and gathers her books, muttering to herself. Seeing the back of her head gives me a prickly thrill in the pit of my stomach. One of her books has landed beyond her. I grab it. It'd be a dangerous move if it were anyone but Jeanette, but I'm better than her, even when I'm not.

She doesn't catch sight of the book until I wave it in front of her face. *Moron.* She tries to snatch it out of my hands, but I back away and hold it out of her reach.

"Give me my book!"

The venom in her voice surprises me a little. I know she hates me, but I don't think I ever disliked Jeanette. I think I liked her. I didn't respect her, but I liked her.

"Who put the meat in my locker?" I demand. She gets uncomfortable all over, clutching her books like they're a security blanket.

"I'm not allowed to talk to you." She's practically sweating. It's really pathetic. "Give me my book back."

"Tell me who put the meat in my locker and I'll give you your book and I'll leave you alone. If you don't, I'll stand here until Anna shows and sees you with me."

"Bruce and Kara," she blabs. "Now give me my book!"

I keep it out of her reach, because I can and because it feels good. Jeanette stamps her foot, and I can't help but grin.

*"Give me my fucking book, Regina!"*

I let her rip it from my grasp and watch her storm her way down the up stairs, and then she stops at the bottom of them and turns to me, her face red.

"I'm telling Anna."

"I'm totally shaking, Jeanette." Wait. "Wait. Tell her—tell her you were talking to me and tell Kara to watch her back, but make *sure* you tell them—"

"Fuck you."

She's gone, she's done, but I'm just getting started.

I jog down the steps, past my locker, down the hall. I can't make a Web site about Kara. I turn down another hallway. I already trashed her locker. Can't do that again. I make my way past people going wherever, and I try to block out their voices and the fact that they're pointing and laughing at me *again*. I can't make a Web site about Anna either. Too obvious. There's no one they'd hate to be locked in a closet with. I turn down another hall, a deserted hall, a familiar hall. This is why I got drunk directly after what happened with Donnie. So I didn't have to feel it, but now I feel it, I feel all of it, and it's too much and I—*Do something do something.*

I push through the door to the storage room and slam it behind me because I don't care, and I grab the box of broken things and throw it against the wall. It explodes.

And then it's quiet.

I press my hand against my forehead. My head is throbbing. I'm breathing like I ran a marathon, and my stomach is churning and my throat is tight and I'm hot. I kick one of the old mats and then I kick it again, and then I bite my arm because I'm going to scream; I'm not going to scream and . . . okay.

It's okay.

My chest caves in, deflates; my heart is calm, my heart is pumping calm. No—not calm. Nothing. I should go back. But I kneel down and press my hands against the cold floor and crawl until I'm against the wall instead. I'll go home and talk to Mom and Dad about finishing out the year—not at school. I can't do this anymore.

I bring my knees up and rest my head against them. I close my eyes. I run my hand over the floor, feeling grit and dust, and I have a problem.

Now that I'm down, I don't want to get up.

I guess I can stay here awhile.

I'm just starting to get into that peaceful, falling kind of place between dozing and actual sleep when the door opens slowly, and some vague alarm goes off inside me—*Oh no, you're caught*—but I don't care until the light from the hallway hits my eyelids and rudely jolts me into wakefulness, and then I do. I look up. Michael is standing in the doorway holding a black garbage bag. He flicks on the light and I wince.

"The stuff from your locker," he says, holding the bag up. He sets it inside the door, which he closes quietly behind him, and then he faces the room. I watch him take it all in. The mess I made. ". . . Are you okay?"

"How did you know I was here?" My tongue feels thick.

"I followed you," he says. "I saw you come in here. I thought I'd give you a minute so I cleaned out your locker. It's clean."

"Thanks," I say.

"I can't believe they did that to you," he says. "I mean, I can, but—"

"Yeah."

He crosses the room and sits beside me, close. His shoulder against my shoulder. I tense and then I relax. It's not like he can reject me twice, because I'm not going to make a move. I'm not saying anything. A few minutes pass, and he clears his throat.

"So what *did* you do to Kara?"

I look at him. He looks at me. I laugh a little, because even though it's not funny, it's not anything like what I thought he was going say.

"Uhm . . ." I bite my lower lip. "Kara couldn't keep up. So we—I mean, *I* told her that a lot. It kind of fucked her up. A lot."

And the rest is history.

"So I guess I deserve this," I add absently.

And then my eyes catch sight of the garbage bag against the wall with all of my ruined things inside of it, and my face dissolves. Don't cry. *Don't cry.* It shouldn't matter at this point. Michael's seen me at my worst, but I press my hand against my eyes, taking short pathetic breaths in and out until I'm choking on air, and all I want to do is tell him about how paralyzing it was in that closet with Donnie and how we weren't always like this and how sick it is, but all I can manage are these six, stilted words: "I-just-want-them-to-stop."

"I can take you home," he says. I shake my head and wipe my eyes. "You can't stay here, Regina. Let me take you home."

"No," I say. I sound like a stubborn little kid. *No.* But I don't want to step into the halls again, because I'm tired of being out there and this feels safe. He gets to his feet and holds his hand out, and I push him away. "*Stop.* Michael, stop it—"

"Remember when I told you my mom wouldn't have hated you, even if she'd known what you'd done? She would've tried to help you." He pauses. "That means something to me." I close my eyes and shake my head. "Please let me help you."

I open my eyes. I take his hand. His fingers close around mine and he helps me to my feet. We end up close and it hurts, because I want to be this close to someone who wants to be this close to me. He doesn't want me.

"You hate me."

"I don't hate you," he says.

I look at him and I think he's telling the truth. Before, I could see it—that he hated me. But now it's not there enough for me to see, if it's there at all, and that's the strangest feeling I've had in a long time.

"Regina," he says. "I don't hate you."

He edges closer until there's no space between us and brings his hands to my face so awkwardly, like this isn't what he set out to do, but now that we're here, he's going to do it all the same. This is a test. This is not a test.

He kisses me. Presses his lips against mine gently, hesitantly, and when I kiss back, he kisses harder, deeper. I feel like he wants me. He brings his hand to my neck and kisses me and kisses me again. I bring my hands around to the back of his neck, his hair tickling past my knuckles, and his fingers drift down to my sides. For a minute, I'm dizzy with how good it feels and how amazing it is that I could have this moment that feels so good.

He's so *nice.*

He brings his mouth to my neck. I shiver and close my eyes, my hands still in his hair. He stops for a second and we stand there, his lips just barely there, and he brings his hands up and gently pushes my collar back so there's more of me for him to kiss and my legs feel sort of weak. His mouth comes back to mine. I bring my hand to his chest.

Steady.

The door flies open, puts a space between us so wide it's like we were never on each other at all. I'm breathing heavily and he's breathing heavily. I squint at the figure in the door, waiting for my eyes to focus.

It's Bruce. He bursts out laughing as his stupid tiny brain registers what he's just seen and what it's seeing now, and I feel my face turn red.

"Jesus Christ," he says. "Are you serious?"

"Fuck off," I tell him, crossing my arms. My head still feels fuzzy with the kiss. I shake it a little, to clear it. "What are you doing here?"

He just smiles and he doesn't say anything, and I get this uneasy feeling that he knew—he knew I was here all along. I glance at Michael, and I think he's thinking the same thing, because he clenches his jaw. Even Bruce notices. He backs off and laughs again and then he goes and he laughs himself down the hall.

"Great," I say. "Now they'll know that we—"

"So?" Michael asks, turning to me. "So what?"

We stare at each other. So they know; so what? I wonder if, even after all this, he understands how fragile good things are in my hands and how many times they've been taken away from me. I lean over and give him an impulsive kiss on the cheek, and then I leave the storage room and he leaves after me.

I wake up wired, and I go to school wired, popping antacids like they're candy. It's been one day and I feel sick, excited, nervous.

It was almost easier when he hated me. I'm used to that.

Hallowell High: Everyone's dressed for the weather.

Michael is waiting for me at my locker. The red door hangs open, a useless empty mouth, waiting to be filled with all I could salvage last night. He straightens when he sees me, and I try to ignore the funny feeling in my stomach, but when he smiles, it gets worse in a good way, and it goes straight to my head in a good way.

"Hi," he says, holding out his hand. His fingers are closed around something I can't see. "I have something for you. Open your hand."

I do. He presses something heavy into it. I look down. A new combination lock.

"Thanks," I say.

"The combination is four, fifteen, thirty, and three."

"Thank you," I repeat.

He moves forward, and then he hesitates and moves back. Whatever's between us is that kind of new. He runs a hand through his hair.

"So I'll see you at lunch," he says. I nod.

He studies me for a good minute and then—he kisses me. Like, right here in the hall. In front of everyone. I feel people milling around us, their voices getting louder the closer they get. Breaking news: My mouth is on Michael Hayden's mouth, and he means it.

I glimpse blond hair. Liz. She turns a corner going to the girls' room. Which means she saw this. Michael pulls away and says, "Okay, good."

"Lunch," I repeat. He nods this time and passes me. I watch him go, and then I turn and head for the washroom because I want to see what she makes of it. When I push through the door, she's coming out of the stall. She glances at me and then runs the water, keeping her eyes on her reflection, and I just stand there keeping my eyes on her.

"What do you want me to say, Regina?" she finally asks.

"I don't know," I say.

"I'm not giving you my blessing," she says.

"I didn't ask for it."

"Then why are you here?" I don't know. She turns off the water and I turn back to the door, and she says, "He doesn't know what he's doing."

"But when he hates me, he knows what he's doing?"

"You really fucked him up, so if—" She shakes her head, like this whole turn of events has been pissing her off since the dawn of time. "You probably don't get it, but if he's giving you a chance, that's a big deal."

I grit my teeth. "I get it."

I wish I'd never come in here at all.

"I don't think you do," she says, looking me up and down. I bite the inside of my cheek but I don't say anything. "But whatever, Regina; use him up."

Some people will never give up on their lack of belief in you. I'm used to that feeling, but for the first time ever, it hurts. Maybe because Michael got past it, and now I'm standing here wondering why she can't and if she ever will.

"Thanks," I say.

"I couldn't talk him out of you."

*I couldn't talk him out of you.* Her voice echoes in my head from class to class, and my stomach aches. When the lunch bell rings, I'm eager to see Michael. I pass Josh in the hall on my way to the cafeteria and keep my eyes straight ahead.

"Are you and Hayden a thing now?" he asks.

I roll my eyes and stop. "What?"

He stops. "Bruce said he caught you two fucking around in a storage room, and now everyone's talking about how you two were making out in the hall earlier. Is it true? Are you with Hayden?"

"It's none of your business."

"If you're making out with him in hallways, it's everyone's business." He looks me over and laughs. "You're not with Hayden. He hates you. Everyone knows he hates you. He feel sorry for you or something? Desperate to get some?"

"Fuck off."

"He must be *really* desperate," he says. "Or maybe you're the desperate one."

"Michael's the best thing that's happened to me."

My cheeks warm instantly. It's one of those insanely stupid-sounding declarations that people laugh at you for, no matter how true it is. But it's true.

Josh laughs at me. "I've noticed a whole lot has changed for you since you decided to hang around with Mr. Mysterious—" I punch him in the shoulder before he can finish, because I can't think of a better or more satisfying way to shut him up. "—Jesus *Christ*, Regina! What is *wrong* with you?"

"What's wrong with *you*? You just stand there and watch every day while Anna makes my life a living hell. Who just sits there and *watches* something like that?"

"*You* did," Josh snaps. "You always did. Her name was Liz, remember? Don't act like you're better than me, Regina. You're not."

"But Michael is," I tell him.

Josh turns red. I know somehow I've hurt him. "Well, maybe your new boyfriend should watch his back."

My stomach lurches and he smirks, satisfied. The threat goes deep. I turn and head for the cafeteria, digging into my pockets for an antacid, trying to understand how I can be this close to fucking everything up already. When I see Michael at the Garbage Table, I'm flooded with relief. He's in one piece.

And he's waiting for me.

I weave around tables and sit across from him. His lunch today—fries and Coke. His Moleskine rests beside him. I just watch him for a minute and I feel like Liz is right. He's really lonely and I fuck things up. Just because he gets to this point where he wants to kiss me doesn't mean I instantly wake up tomorrow brave. I'm afraid of what Josh said.

"What's wrong?" he asks.

I shake my head. "Nothing." Everything.

He doesn't look like he believes me, but then, thankfully, embarrassingly, my stomach makes this awful hungry gurgle and he hears it. He raises an eyebrow.

"Hungry?" he asks.

I wave a hand. "I'll eat when I get home."

"Let me get you something," he says, nodding at the lunch line, and I start telling him how I can't eat in this place, and he interrupts. "I'll get you something small."

Like that would make a difference. But he gets up and goes. I watch him go. My gaze drifts over to the center table, where Josh is leaning over and whispering something in Anna's ear. His mouth moves from her ear, grazing her cheek, and meets her lips; I don't want Michael on their radar.

I turn back to the table. Michael's trusty Moleskine is resting next to his tray.

I want to read it.

He's standing in line and he's not looking my way. I know I shouldn't do this, but I have to do this, and I don't have a lot of time to have an ethical debate about it right now. I grab it and flip it open, flip past page after page, searching for my name. I glimpse words like *Mom, Dad, hate, yesterday, I, stupid school*, and all of them mean something, but they're not what I want.

I skip to the end, and then—

*Might not last.*

I know it's about me. It's dated yesterday. It says I'm not a sure thing—like I could really fuck this up. I press my index fingers against the words, as if I could feel what he was feeling when he wrote it, but it's just ink on paper. I flip ahead, but there's nothing. I set the Moleskine back where it was and wait for him to come back, and I guess there's some truth in it. I don't think I can divide myself so completely between him and Anna.

Someone will get hurt.

*Maybe your new boyfriend should watch his back.*

I look up at the center table. Anna is watching me, interested in a way that makes me sick. I spot Michael winding his way back to the table, a small container of yogurt in his hand, and I am overwhelmed with how much more I like him than I hate my ex-friends.

But I don't know what to do about it. I don't think I'm that brave.

*Do something.*

After school, I end up at the park.

Small-town entertainment. Kid explosion in the summer. Everyone vies for a shot at the swings and the monkey bars and the playhouse and the slides and the metal merry-go-round thing that some little girl supposedly severed a limb on years ago. Today the place is empty, save for the snack wagon, which doesn't pack up until the first snow flies. I buy some greasy fries from the guy holding the place down, drown them in ketchup, and eat them on top of the monkey bars.

A light breeze pushes the swings back and forth. I finish off the fries and try to enjoy the quiet. It's easy to be out here: I'm not surrounded.

After a long time, two separate cars pull into the parking lot. No one I recognize. Two soccer moms step out of each car, dragging two little girls with them, respectively. Must be a play date.

They stay to the far side of the park, away from the big toys. I watch them and feel a sense of relief when I see the girls don't have much interest in each other. They pick separate spaces of grass and focus on the dolls they've brought with them while their moms talk. I hope they stay away from each other, because odds are good one of them has the making of a total bitch and the other will become that bitch's total bitch.

Because that's how it works. Mostly.

I lean back, hooking my legs over the bars and snaking through the spaces between them until I'm hanging upside down.

"Mommy, look at that!" One of the girls shrieks. "I want to do that!"

"That's dangerous honey," her mom says. "Why don't you go play with Casey? You two can play dolls with each other. . . ."

*That's* dangerous.

I stay upside down until I feel like my head is going to burst and I ease back up. I lie across the bars and bundle my coat under my head like a pillow. After an hour or so, the women leave with their daughters. The temperature drops and the light shifts.

I stare at the sky and wait for it to come to me.

Truce.

Truce.

I wake up and that word is in my head.

This morning—a pale pink antacid with coffee. Truce. Dad goes through the whole paper, and I'm still debating it. He leaves. Mom is running late, looking for her car keys. I feel guilty watching her. She just wants to be a good mother, and it's weird and sad to me how we're all in some small ways trying to be good.

"I broke up with Josh," I tell her. I don't know why. "A while ago."

Her head snaps up, eyes wide and surprised, and then they glaze over like she finally understands everything that's been going on. She takes this one little piece of the puzzle and puts it into the wrong picture.

"I'm sorry, Regina," she says. "That's too bad."

"Not really." I shrug. "He was useless."

"They sometimes are," she says, amused.

She gives me a kiss on the cheek and leaves. I sit at the table for as long as I can stretch it out and then I grab my book bag and walk to school.

Truce.

I'm not stupid. I know it's dumb and impossible, but it's all I've got. It's dumb and impossible but it's also grown-up and brave. Not the easy thing to do. And maybe Anna will see that and she'll be so shocked and amazed that I asked her—no one's asked for a truce before—that she'll let me have it, and then I'll tell Michael and it will get back to Liz, and Liz will be impressed, and we all untie ourselves from this Regina, and then I get to be the one that's happy and braver and like . . .

Better.

Time passes too quickly when you're getting ready to do something you don't want to do. The morning and afternoon disappear, and I keep trying to figure out how I'm going to do this, but you can't really plan anything when you deal with Anna.

"What's going on?" Michael asks me at lunch. I'm jiggling my knee under the table like a spaz, and my palms are slimy with sweat.

"Nothing," I tell him. I want it to be a surprise. "I'm just . . ." I trail off and offer him a feeble smile. "Monday."

That's all I need to say.

I skip out on my last class and wait for Anna at her Benz. I swallow a couple antacids. I keep wiping my hands on my jeans. Every time I inhale, my whole chest tingles, and by the time the last bell rings, I can't breathe. I can do this. I tense and watch students shove each other out the front door—I duck out of sight as Michael gets into his Saturn and drives away—until, eventually, *they* emerge— the four of them together.

I can almost see myself wedged between Anna and Kara. Kara always kept her distance, slightly removed, because I told her to. I watch Marta and Jeanette break off for Jeanette's car. For a second, I think if I could do it all over again, I'd want to be one of those two, because they don't matter. But I'd never do it all over again.

Kara points me out to Anna. Anna gives me the dirtiest look

when they reach her Benz. I straighten. My fingers curl and a famil-iar hot feeling spreads through me. I try to bury it.

I need to be beyond that. Now.

"Get," Anna says, pointing across the parking lot, "away from my car."

"I need to—" It comes out sounding like there are hands around my throat. I cough and try again. "I need to talk to you."

Anna crinkles her nose. "How about . . ."

"No?" Kara suggests.

Anna shoves me out of the way and pulls her keys from her purse.

"I need to talk to you about—" Kara rounds the car, rolling her eyes, and I just blurt the words out: "I want you to leave me alone."

Anna and Kara exchange a glance and laugh.

"I mean a truce," I blurt out.

They freeze. Anna's eyes travel from the keys to her hand to the car to Kara, who leans over the hood, shocked. The moment passes quickly. Anna snorts and unlocks her door. She opens it. Kara stays where she is, but I'm not appealing to Kara.

I grab Anna's door and block her path.

"Fuck off, Regina."

This is the closest I've been to her since I slapped her, and she looks as angry as she did then. My heart gets all tangled up in my stomach, and my mouth is a desert. I scrape my tongue along my lips.

"There's no way we're going to be friends with you," Kara says.

"I'm not asking you for your friendship, you idiot. I'm asking you for a truce."

*"No,"* Kara says, at the same time Anna says, *"Why?"*

At least the suggestion is unprecedented enough to capture An-na's attention, like I thought it might be. I doubt it will be enough to capture her heart. Especially with Kara standing right there. I wish I could push Kara out of this picture and off a cliff.

"I want you off my back," I say. "Why else do you think?"

"No," Kara says. "We're not—"

Anna holds her hand up, silencing Kara. She inclines her head for me to continue.

"We're graduating soon," I say. "I'm tired of this. Truce."

"If you were really tired of this, you wouldn't keep pushing back."

"What am I supposed to do?" I demand. Neither of them says what they're thinking. "Oh, so I'm just supposed to stand there and let you—"

"Yes. After what you did to me," Anna says, "*yes.*"

Anna will never believe what really happened with Donnie. And now I'm the one who has to give. I'm conceding to the girls who locked me in a closet with a guy who tried to rape me.

I didn't think this out. I don't think I can do this.

"Forget it." I raise my hands. "Just—forget it."

"Wait," Anna says. She sizes me up. "If you want a truce, I want something for it."

"No." Her eyes widen. Anna has never heard me say the word to her before. I've never seen her consider a truce, though, either, so I don't want to shoot myself in the foot. I eye her warily. "What do you want, Anna?"

The question stumps her. There's nothing I have that she wants. I get a glimmer of hope in the pit of my gut. If she doesn't think of anything, I could walk away from this intact.

"Give it to me," Kara says. "Anna, give it to me."

"Fuck off, Kara," I say.

Anna's eyes light up, and I hate myself for giving that away. She never takes her eyes off me as she tells Kara, "Okay, K. I'll leave it to you."

Kara doesn't even try to build to it, doesn't want to torture me or list a slew of horrible, degrading things she could force me to do in the name of a truce. Instead, she leans across the car eagerly and says, "Apologize."

She's trembling, she wants it so bad. I guess I can give it to her. For Michael. I open my mouth and wait for the words to come— they don't mean anything—but they stay stuck inside, like being stuck in a closet with Donnie Henderson, like me being stuck in a room with Donnie Henderson. *It wouldn't be so hard to hide the bruises.*

"You're joking."

"Those are my terms."

My mouth moves, but nothing comes out. I want to hurt her. I want to hurt her for having the balls to ask. Kara smiles and says, "Fine. See you tomorrow."

"Wait—"

They're only words. I'll just say them even though she locked me in a fucking closet with Donnie Henderson. *Don't. Don't freak out. Let her have this.*

"I'm"—*not sorry*—"I—Kara—"

I think of all those notes that are still on my desk and try to inspire the same guilt that came over me when I saw the one from Liz, but it's impossible. Kara is my legacy, and I don't regret that because she deserves everything I did to her, and if she didn't *then*, she does now. I *can't* let her have this.

"This is fascinating," Anna says dryly. "But I'd like to go home now."

"I fucking *hate* you Kara." It explodes from my mouth, and now *I'm* the one trembling, because that's how bad I want to tell her. "You're pathetic, you've always been pathetic, and *everything* I said to you came out of Anna's mouth first. It's *hilarious* that you have so little self-respect you'd get me kicked out of our group so you could hang around the bitch that never gave a damn about you in the first place."

"Blah, blah." Kara opens the car door and gets inside. "This is so over."

But Anna stays where she is. She stares at me in amazement. "You don't know when to give up, do you? Even Liz knew—"

"*Don't* say her name."

"Oh, don't act so hurt," Anna says. "You should've thanked me, Regina. I did it for you. You were *that* important to me."

"You're sick," I say.

"But you're the one who sold Liz out so we could stay friends. You let me drive her to the edge. You never once told me to stop. If I'm sick, what does that make you?"

"That's *your* legacy, Anna. What you did to Liz. No matter what you do next, all everyone in this school is going to remember is that you're a horrible fucking person."

"Like I give a damn what these losers think."

"Kara's lying to you. She's making a fool out of you."

She laughs. "That'll be the day. Anyway, see you tomorrow, Regina."

She gets in the car and burns rubber out of the parking lot.

teenylinks.com/28ccyz

:)

—K

I stare at the e-mail for a half hour, trying to figure out
what to do. Kara's fed the original link into a URL alias site. If I
click it, it could send me anywhere. And since the link is from
Kara, I know I won't walk away from whatever it leads to un-
scathed. A computer virus, maybe. Skeevy porn or worse—it's total bait.

I have to take it. I back up the computer first. That takes longer
than I want it to. The e-mail sits in my inbox the whole time, waiting
to be read.

I click the link.

When it takes me to the IH8RA page, I feel a sense of relief. I've
seen this stupid page. I almost forget it was there. I've like grown
beyond it, and it's—

Grown.

**THINGS YOU DIDN'T KNOW REGINA THOUGHT ABOUT YOU AND
YOU DIDN'T KNOW ABOUT HER . . . (CLICK HERE TO READ ENTRY)
NEW PHOTOS IN THE PHOTO ALBUM!**

The comments are bursting, and every one of them has something to say about the new dirt on me. I search for some kind of indication of what I can expect, because I'm too afraid to click the links. I'll have to, though. If most of the school knows what's behind them, I have to, so when I walk through the doors tomorrow—

I'll know.

One comment steals all the air from my lungs.

**I hope she fucking dies.**

It's from some freshman I don't really know named Katie Langden.

Someone I don't really know wants me to die.

I scroll up the page and start with the photos. Every embarrassing moment Anna managed to capture on camera is on display. I try to make peace with the fact that at least half of the school has now seen me at my worst. It's okay. Everyone at school has been the person who passed out next to the toilet; they just didn't have Anna hovering over them with a Nikon when they were. Bad hair days. Bad fashion choices. This is ugliness, but it's nothing. It's—totally mortifying.

I click away.

*Things You Didn't Know . . .*

Click. I stare at my handwriting. My notes. All scanned in. A gallery. Anna's ammunition. I couldn't get them all. I tried. I'd always try to end our notes on stupid, innocuous questions, something she had to answer and send back so I could have them, but sometimes I was careless. . . .

I scroll through them, numb. I'd forgotten the time we tore apart all the girls in our English class. Names down one side, physical flaws down the other. It was a group effort, but I was secretary, so now it gets pinned on me. All the fat thighs, big asses, crater faces, lisps. These girls are still at school, and I have to face them tomorrow.

*Guys I'd never sleep with and why.* The companion list, also in my handwriting. Written on a boring, sweltering hot day in math class. Ernie Sanders heads it up. Quiet and shy, future astronaut, he tutored me in tenth grade, and my handwriting reduces him to the size—or lack of size—of his penis. I called Carter Anders a Cro-Mag.

I thought it was fun at the time.

Some notes are one-sided conversations, little commentaries on people I didn't know enough to like. No one who looks at the scanned pieces of paper will notice the way they're ripped. Anna's replies, which were always usually more scathing, are hacked off the bottom.

And that's not all: My secrets are there. Precious thoughts I committed to paper and trusted her with because I was stupid. Worrying about my first time. Whether or not it would hurt. How useless I think my parents are. Why I like it in the dark.

I wrote it all down.

I stop breathing. My head pounds. The screen starts to gray out. I didn't actually think you could get so mad you could lose the room, but here I am, gripping the edge of my desk and trying to bring myself back enough so that I can click the Report Abuse link and then—

Fuck a truce. Fuck it.

Revenge comes into my head fully formed, so simple and so perfect I don't know why I didn't think of it before. Anna always said to stay above the hate. She's obsessive about it, because she knows everyone hates her. Don't let them know you know. Don't let them see it on your face. Don't be weak. *Never let them know your weaknesses.*

But I've always known her weaknesses.

I haven't even cooled by the time I've created the fake e-mail and the fake YourSpace account. So easy. My fake name is Alison Raft, and Alison Raft wants to join the IH8RA group. Join, join. Don't get mad, get even.

I have to wait for Kara or whoever heads up the group—it has to be Kara—to approve me. That takes an hour, but I've got the time. As soon as it's done, I find the option that lets me send out a mass message to the inboxes of every member of my anti-fan club. Everyone in school.

I get to work.

**TOMORROW AT LUNCH REGINA AFTON IS GOING TO GET A BIG SURPRISE, AND WE NEED YOUR HELP TO MAKE IT HAPPEN!**

*That* will ensure the e-mail gets opened.

And then I just type. I don't even have to think. I write about Anna's dad leaving the family for someone twenty years younger and how Anna had to beg for regular visits. I write about the first time Kara had sex—a vacation in Cancun. He was ten years older. The diet pills, the purging, the wig. Everyone knows that, but why not rehash? And the drunken handjob Anna gave Bruce in the ninth grade. How she thought he was small. The chastity ring Kara's father gave her after she lost the weight. How Donnie passed out the first time he had sex with Anna, because he was so wasted. I write down every doubt and insecurity, the dumb stuff, the mortifying stuff. Things I guarded with my life and that don't mean anything to me anymore. I give it all away for free.

It's crude, simple, and effective.

But the most beautiful thing about it is, this is *nothing* compared to the work they've put into destroying me. Nothing. I don't even have to break a sweat. Anna's been so untouched for years that she'll wake up tomorrow and her world will end.

Thank you, Anna. For being so perfect and so ugly.

I sign my name to the e-mail—my real name—and then I send it to everyone.

# tuesday

**When I wake up, I head for the computer first.**

The YourSpace page is gone.

My first victory. It may be gone, but the e-mail isn't. It's in everyone's inboxes, waiting to be read. If it hasn't been read already. I can be certain of two people who *did* read it, and the thought turns me into a face full of teeth. I can't wait to go to school and see what I've wrought. Damage control will be spectacular. Anna won't have time to think up ways to retaliate, because she'll be too frantic trying to keep herself above this, recovering her reputation. *If* she can recover it.

What a beautiful *if*.

Michael calls and asks if I want a ride. Yes, a million times *yes*. I get dressed for school and sit at the breakfast table with my parents and I *eat*. A piece of toast dripping with butter. It tastes fantastic. I can't believe how great my stomach feels. I can't believe that's all it took. Next thing, maybe I'll get off the antacids.

I can't wait to see Michael. When I spot his Saturn making its way up the street, I can't even play it cool. I run outside before he pulls into the driveway, and then I jerk the door open and practically throw myself inside.

"Hi," I say.

"Hi," Michael says, surprised. I'm too cheerful, but that's how *good* I feel, how happy I am. I should try to get a hold on it, but I don't want to get a hold on it. I just want to *be* it. He pulls out of the driveway. I'm not sure whether I should tell him now or wait. Wait. It'll be a surprise. I lean across the seat and kiss him.

Michael smiles at me and I look away, biting my lip. I feel sick when Hallowell High comes into sight, but it's a five-minutes-before-curtain kind of sick.

We pull into the parking lot. Michael unbuckles his seatbelt, taking his time, but I can't wait for him. I get out of the car and scope out the entrance. They're not there and I want to squeal. *They aren't there*; the doors are clear. People are free to come and go as they please. *I sent them into hiding.* Me. Wow.

I shrug my book bag over my shoulder, and Michael and I walk into school. I'm five feet past the doors when Chelsea Redcliff grabs my arm. I jerk away and edge close to Michael. Chelsea was the crater face in that long list of girls on the YourSpace page. Or the small chest. I can't remember. She's neither of these things now, but if she's angry, I want someone between us.

"Did you send it? That was really you?"

I nod. "Yeah."

"So it's all true?"

I nod again and she stands there, shocked. If I can't see this moment on Anna's face, this is really the next best thing. I watch Chelsea's mouth quirk as she enjoys this victory for . . . everyone. Michael divides his gaze between both of us.

"You're a total bitch," she says in an admiring tone, and then she hurries into school so she can spread the word: *It was Regina, and it's all true.*

"What was that?" Michael asks when she's gone. I can't find the words to answer him, so I duck my head and make my way down the hall. I'm immediately stared at, which is nothing new, but this is different. Even he notices. "What's going on . . . ?"

Bruce slams into Michael then. Hard. Michael manages to stay upright, but his book bag hits the floor and his books go flying. Before I can tell Bruce he's an asshole, he's on me, pointing fingers, red-faced. And I can't help it: I smile.

"You're a fucking *bitch*, Afton."

He kicks Michael's books, sending them into the lockers. A modest crowd witnesses the whole scene, and soon the halls are buzzing, but the buzzing sounds very, very confused.

"Okay, tell me what's going on," Michael says, shoving the books back into his bag. He catches sight of something beyond me. I half-turn and spot Liz. "Don't make me find out secondhand."

"I did something," I tell him. He doesn't even know what I did, but he gets this look on his face, like it can't be good even though it's good, it's great, it's the best. I open my mouth to tell him, but then before I can answer some sophomore I don't know passes us, pointing me out to some freshman I don't know. "*That's* Regina Afton! Last night—"

This is so awesome.

Five minutes before lunch, I detour into the girls' room and try to get it together. It used to be I had to prep myself not to look so miserable when I walked through the halls.

Now I have to try not to look so high.

It's a total high. I stare at my reflection in the mirrors. I haven't seen myself this happy in ages. I run the water really cold and dab at my face and hands. I'm hot.

One of the stall doors opens and startles me. I bite the inside of my cheek hard to keep the smile off my face. I'd love to smug this out all over school, but I can't. Not yet. And it's Liz, so I don't feel like smiling anymore anyway. She stares at me in the mirror and I turn the water off. I dry my hands and head for the door.

"I can't believe you had it in you," she says at my back.

I pause. "Thanks."

"That wasn't a compliment."

"Nothing I do is good enough for you." I face her. "That's okay. But they got what they deserved."

"And what did *you* deserve?" she asks. "Charie called me and said there was this e-mail in her inbox. Well done, I guess."

"Is that what everyone thinks?" I ask.

"Oh, they still hate you," she says. "But they hate Anna more."

I leave her and go to the cafeteria. The center table is devoid of girls. Josh, Henry, and Bruce are there, trying to uphold what's left of their popularity. Without Anna, they're nothing. I find Michael at the back, as usual.

"They've been dogging me all day," he says, nodding at the guys. I take my seat across from him. "Every time I turn around, one of them is there."

I turn, expecting to see some Sinister Group Glare being leveled at us, but the three of them are hunched over their food.

"Have they said anything to you?" I ask. He shakes his head. "They probably just want to tell Anna they weren't totally useless today."

And then I look again. I can't help it. They're just there, and the table is totally dead, and it's amazing because I did that and no one's ever done that before. I turn back to Michael. The bell separated us before I could find out how he felt about it, and the way he's staring at me, I'm not sure I want to find out.

"Smile," he says after a minute.

"What?"

"I can tell you want to do it," he says.

I flush and look away. "You say that like it's a bad thing." When he doesn't immediately reply, it gets my back up. "They deserve it, Michael. You can't tell me they don't."

"You're going to get your ass kicked," he says.

I can feel eyes on me from every direction, but there's something different about it. Like, maybe they hate me, but I'm cool. It feels cool. This is mine.

"No, I'm not," I say, and then I point. "Look at that table, Michael. I have them."

"But why would you want them?" he asks.

It's not an accusation; it's worse. There's discomfort in his voice and . . . disappointment. It hurts in a weird way because I don't know what that means. *They didn't deserve it?* He can't think that. They deserved it. They *deserve* it. I could do it again and again and again and they'd deserve it each time. For what they did to me.

"Why do you want to make me feel bad about this?"

"I don't," he says. "I just don't get why you have to feel so *good* about it."

"Oh, I'm sorry," I say. "Is this too *Anna* for you?"

He leans forward and says very slowly, "I don't want you to get hurt."

I turn back to the table. Josh is gone. I wonder if he's gone to see her. She won't get her reputation back enough to hurt me. She can't. I ate *breakfast* today. That has to be a good omen. I smile at the thought, and when I turn back to Michael again, he's just looking more and more weirded out. Like it *is* too Anna for him.

The day passes in that odd, tense way a day does when you're with someone who is mad at you and you don't fully understand why. It reminds me of Anna, because she used to do that to all of us a lot. Seize up, freeze out. It was always scary.

I'm mad at Michael for reminding me of that.

Still, somehow, we end up in his room.

We end up in his room on his bed.

But not like that.

We are side by side and quiet. He's on his back, staring at the ceiling, and I'm on my side, staring at him. This is the kind of closeness that comes in at you from all sides, the kind that begs you to move and do something before it traps you and you can't do anything at all. Are we mad at each other? Is this a fight? I take a look around the room. It's as sparse as the rest of the house. There's a photograph of his mother on the wall. It's really strange and sad. All I have of her is a memory in a chair in an office. In this photo, she is every inch a mother. No doctor showing on her. She's sitting at a picnic table smiling at a man. Michael's father, maybe. She looks happy.

"I'm sorry," I tell him.

He turns to me. "What?"

"I made things really bad for you."

"My mom died," he says. "Things were already bad."

"I just made them worse."

It's quiet for a long time.

"Yeah."

He reaches over and his hand drifts up my side until it reaches my face, and then his palm is on my chin, but he's hesitant, and I feel bad. I understand it.

But I don't want to understand it.

"Don't be mad at me," I say. "It was the only way it could have happened."

"Really?" he asks, and before I can say anything, he runs his thumb over my lips and I close my eyes. My eyes are still closed when he kisses me. And then he stops, and when I open my eyes, the same close-distance that was between us before is there again.

I sit up and stare out the window, my back to him. Michael's bedroom overlooks the street. His house is a strange quiet. There's no calm in it, just this total emptiness. I watch the wind stir the last of some leaves off a tree across the road.

"Where's your dad?" I ask. "What does he do? He's never home. . . ."

"Lawyer."

"Why didn't you tell your mom about what we did to you?" I turn to him. "You didn't know I was seeing her. You could've told her."

"She listened to people for a living."

"Do you wish you'd told her?"

He shrugs. "I started keeping that journal. It's—"

He doesn't finish, but I know what he's not saying. It makes him feel closer to her. I think of him carrying it everywhere. School. His car. Home. Writing incessantly just to make some kind of connection to a dead woman. His mom.

"I'm sorry," I say again. "But I'm glad I did it to them."

"Okay," he says. It's not enough.

"What do you think?" I ask him. "They deserved it, right?"

"I think . . ." he trails off. "I think some girls are just . . . fucked up."

He eases himself across the bed. He doesn't say he's not—that he's not mad at me or that it's not weird anymore. He might be. It is. So I reach out and push his hair back from his face, and then he kisses me again, and it's like he just lets it go, just for this.

I think.

He kisses my neck and he kisses my mouth. We curl up on his bed together, a tangle of arms and legs. His hand slides up my shirt, and I kiss him and I kiss him again.

I'm not one of those girls.

The Formerly Fearsome Foursome is still nowhere to be found for the second day in a row. They're just gone. I'm still dying to see it on their faces, but I'll settle for this not-insignificant change to the landscape. Michael and I separate at the front doors.

"See you at lunch," he tells me, heading down the hall.

When I get to my locker, there's a note tucked in it. I know who it's from instantly. Anna or Kara. Some small part of me is excited to get it, because no matter what it says, they sent it from a place that is now officially beneath me.

I set my bag down, grab the note, and unfold it. But it's not from Anna.

Or Kara.

The handwriting isn't immediately familiar to me. It's a single line on a piece of paper that has a photocopied quality about it.

*I hate it here.*

Michael.

His name floats into my head for no reason at all.

I turn, expecting to find him behind me. He's not. But—

Oh.

I try to work it out. Why do I have this. Why was it in my locker.

At first, I think it's a gift from him. Something so important and private—he wants me to see it, wants to share it, but he wouldn't, not even now, because that's . . . his mom. I flip the page over and see another line scrawled across the back:

*Underneath the water fountain outside of Hartnett's.*

The handwriting is deliberately warped.

This isn't bad. Not yet. I crumple the paper and rush for Hartnett's room. I'm halfway down the hall when I realize I've left my book bag sitting in front of my locker, but I don't care. The bell feels like it could go soon, so I leave it.

This is more important.

Ellen Pines is taking the longest drink of her life when I finally reach the fountain, and my head is pounding, swimming. I wait and wait and I'm about to shove her out of the way, when she stands, wipes her mouth, and goes. I run my hand along the porcelain underside until I find the next piece of paper taped to it.

I rip it off and unfold it.

*I think I liked being an Unstable Freak better before she died.*
*I hate everyone in this school, but I want to tell them about her.*

I somehow manage to keep the guilt that's invading every space inside of me from turning into tears. This is so private. I flip the paper over and it directs me to the fountain outside of Holt's office. No one's there. I rip the note off and unfold it. I don't want to read it. But I do.

> *These people all look the same. They walk the same, wear the same type of clothes, talk the same. Nothing that comes out of their mouths is important.*
> *These people are wasters.*

It leads me to the fountain on the second floor. It's bad.

> *I'm the antichrist with the anger-management problem. That's the latest.*
> *Everyone here is afraid. It's sort of amazing in a really dumb way. Liz says it's her fault. I like Liz. She's better than most of what's walking the halls.*

I shove my hand into my pocket and find an antacid, and then I shove it into my mouth and chew. The next note sends me back to the fountain on the first floor, right by the entrance. I unfold it.

> **I hate it here.**

Even the poor quality of the photocopy can't hide how hard Michael wrote these words. The ink bleeds out, stressed edges around the final sentence. I can't picture him this way. Hurt and angry and ready to explode—like me. He worked so hard to make sure no one ever saw it. At the fountain beside the lab, the next paper reads this:

> *I need a reason.*

I close my eyes and flip the note over. Open them.

*Storage room off the gym.*

The bell rings. I make a run for it. The storage room off the gym. Michael's journal. They have Michael's journal. They dogged him all day yesterday. Why didn't I pay attention? I should've known. *I should've known.* When I reach the storage room, there's one last note taped to the door. I rip it off. I don't need to read it.

I push the door open.

Anna.

"Where's the notebook?" I demand.

"Close the door, Regina," she says calmly. "We need to talk."

"Give me the fucking notebook *now*, Anna."

"It's already back in Michael's hands. He didn't even know it was gone. Now close the door, Regina, so we can talk."

I close the door. "Give me the photocopies then."

She crosses her arms and looks me up and down slowly. That look. Like I'm not good enough to be acknowledged by her. Even after all this. And then the reality of the situation hits me full on, sinking into my bones, making me step back. I don't understand how she's standing here and looking at me like—

"How—" I can't even finish the question.

"You really didn't think I'd just sit around and stare at my hands, did you? Just let you have it?" Anna raises an eyebrow. "That's more *your* style, Regina."

I shake my head. "No—"

"I would've gotten bored with you by now if you'd backed off. I can spray-paint your locker, lock you in storage rooms, ruin your things, broadcast your secrets all over the Internet, and I can make everyone hate you twice as much as they used to, and you *still* haven't learned." She cocks her head to the side. "Right after your e-mail went out, I started brainstorming. That's the trick: Don't waste time. I wanted to figure out how to bury you so far into the ground, you'd *finally* get it *and* never bother me again. Except it was harder than I thought it'd be, because the problem with you is you don't seem to care about what happens to you anymore."

I bite the inside of my cheek so hard there's blood. I let the coppery taste reach my tongue and focus on it. Anna has Michael's journal.

*She has his journal.*

"I was stumped, but then Josh said you'd probably care about what happened to Michael. I guess . . . he's the best thing that's ever happened to you?" She grins, laughing a little as she watches my own words turn my face a ghostly shade of white. "So cute."

"Anna, don't—"

"And *then*," she says over me, "Josh reminded me about Michael's notebook that he always carries around. His journal?"

"Anna—"

"First, I thought we should try to get our hands on it, because maybe there was something in it about *you* we could use. I was skeptical that Hayden had anything interesting to say, but after Bruce got it . . ." She laughs. "And what kind of moron leaves their *journal* in their *car*, by the way? Anyway, after Bruce got it, I was riveted from page one. Michael's very sensitive, did you know?"

"That's a trait you find in people who have souls," I manage.

Her face changes. She's angry, still smarting from what I did to her.

"And how do you think he'd feel if the contents of his *soul* were plastered all over this school? Do you think that would bother him? Given everything he's written, I think it'd bother me, if I were him. He doesn't have much good to say about the people in this school."

"So? Michael doesn't care what people here think of him."

"But would he care if they knew he was so distraught about his dead mother he wanted to die? Like, kill himself? Not that he ever came right out and *said* it, but it's there. It's so obvious."

My brain tries to process Michael that far gone and alone because of—me. And I knew it. It's not like Liz ever told me, but when it's vague, when no one's telling you exactly what you did, it's different. It makes it easier.

"Seriously!" Anna says, relishing the stunned look on my face. "I mean, even *I* didn't think he was *that* depressed! He hid it well, huh? Not like Liz. I always got this vibe from her."

"This is a new low, Anna, even for you."

"Well, I don't *want* to do it, but—"

"I'll tell him. I'll just tell him. No fun for you if I get there first—"

"You tell him and I'll take *this* to Holt." Anna digs into her pocket and hands me another folded piece of paper. I don't want it, but she keeps her hand out until I take it. "*That* was my favorite entry."

My hands are shaking. I don't want her to see them shaking. I have to wait until I feel steady enough to read it.

It's a single line.

*I want to kill everyone in this stupid school.*

"You don't even need to read between the lines for *that* one," Anna says. "No room for interpretation. It's sort of poetic, isn't it? *'I want to kill everyone in this stupid school.'* Strong sentiment. Dangerous sentiment."

I swallow. "So?"

"The first half of his journal is basically about a crazy, depressed boy with a dead mother who hates everyone in this school so much he wants to *kill* them. In this post-Columbine age, you know the rules, Reg." She nods at the paper. "We're supposed to report any warning signs we see. His journal is officially grounds for expulsion . . . probably a hell of a lot of therapy. They could put him away for this."

"No—he's not—I know Michael and he's not—"

He's not like that anymore.

"*You* know Michael," she points out. "Nobody else here does. In fact, what everyone here *thinks* they know about Michael pretty much supports the kind of picture I'm painting. And whose fault is that, by the way? Oh, right. Yours. Well, and mine. But I'll let you take most of the credit for that one."

"He didn't do anything to you," I choke out.

"Well, at first I thought I might be pushing it," she agrees, "but it turns out Michael's not my biggest fan. It's all in his journal: I'm destined to be a future trophy wife who's catatonic all the time because I'm always on pills to dull the pain of my life."

I go completely numb. My pulse stops spazzing, my heart stills.

I stare at the paper in my hand.

*I want to kill everyone in this stupid school.*

"What do you want?" I ask slowly.

She sighs. "Definitely not a truce. You don't get away with what you did to me. You get to suffer for it."

"Just tell me."

"We're reconciling!" She claps her hands. "That's what everyone gets to think! Anna and Regina—best friends again! Can you imagine the looks on everyone's faces when we walk into school together tomorrow? Any respect you earned from your YourSpace e-mail stunt will be instantly gone, and everyone will be so distracted by this insane turn of events, they'll forget all about it. They'll think I must be pretty good if I can get *you* back into the fold, and let's face it, I am. And you—" She grins. "You, Regina, will act like you love it."

I'm shaking my head *no*, but she just keeps talking.

"But really, I'll own you, and Michael is dead to you. You will drop him, with no explanations, nothing. He'll have to sit there trying to figure it out until he gives up and hates you all over again."

I'll tell him.

I'll get out of this storage room and I'll tell him.

Anna studies me. It must be all over my face, because she says, "If I think you've tipped him off, I'll plaster his journal all over school and take it to Holt. If you refuse to drop him, I'll do the same."

My heart stills. Expulsion. Those pages all over school. His grief. His secrets. His ruin. I can't let that happen.

"That means whatever happens to Michael is your fault," Anna says, reading my mind. "And even if he *does* find out the truth, do you think he'd forgive you for putting him through this bullshit? He's already forgiven you for a lot. It wasn't easy for him to be with you, you know. He put that in his journal, too."

"He did?" I whisper.

Anna closes her eyes briefly, basking in this moment. This is Anna at her finest. This is the Anna everyone is afraid of. The Anna I'm afraid of.

She opens her eyes. "Didn't you read the entry I taped to the door?"

I clench my hands into fists. "I hate you so much."

"You did it to yourself." She nudges me out of the way to get to the door and hesitates. "He's really sweet, though, isn't he? Anyway, I'll see you tomorrow."

I dig into my pocket for the entry she was talking out. I unfold it and read it.

And then I start to cry.

*Weird month. The kind of emotional evolution she'd be proud of.*
*It's hard, but—I like her. I think it's going to be good.*

The bell rings. I leave the storage room and keep walking until I'm pushing my way through the front doors. I can't risk Michael seeing me like this, because he'll ask and I'll be weak and I'll tell him, and then Anna will find out and ruin him again, and I can't do that to him, I can't, I can't, *I can't*. I hit the parking lot, gasping, aching. Stupid, ugly tears, all over my face.

I *almost* had them.

I've never felt a more painful miss in my life.

**I go home.**

Anna calls nine hours later.

"Skirt and cardigans tomorrow," she says. "Thought you'd want to know."

Skirts and cardigans.

My throat is all closed up. I try to swallow down my morning coffee and I try to take an antacid but I can't do either, and my parents are just sitting there, and I can't stand it, and I don't know what to do with myself, so I head for school.

My outfit feels stiff and gross, and I can't stop picturing his face when he sees me in it—a fashion clone. The school parking lot is completely empty. I position myself in front of the doors and wait, the familiarity of it suffocating me, until I find myself inside, in the washroom, hunched over a toilet, dry heaving.

Because there's nothing in my stomach to puke up.

I lean against the door and press a shaking hand against my mouth. I could cry, but I'm afraid if I start, I won't stop. I shove an antacid in my mouth and chew it and then try to get it down with a little spit. I can't do this.

*I can't do this.*

Those four words over and over again in my head while time creeps by and the school fills. School noises leech in through the walls, and it eats me up. I take a deep breath and fumble with the door, but I can't open it.

The bell rings. I miss my grand entrance.

I stay in the stall.

I'm going to stay in this stall. I wedge myself against the door, close my eyes, and I stay still until I'm uncomfortable, and even then I don't move.

If I'm not moving, nothing bad is happening.

Every so often people come in, and then the bell rings again and there's that surge before the next period. I listen to girls talk at the sinks, over stalls, and they peter out, and it's quiet again. It stays quiet for a long time, until the door opens and I hear footsteps cut across the room. A stall door is pushed open and then another and another, until it's the one next to mine, and then it's mine. But I've locked it and it doesn't give.

"Get out." It's Marta. "Now."

"No," I say.

"Okay, let's end this now." Kara. "Anna keeps those pages really close, Regina."

I open the door. Marta and Kara exchange a glance and a smile. I catch sight of my reflection in the mirror. My skin looks waxy, pale.

"Lunch in five," Kara says.

I push past them and head straight for the sink. I run the tap hot and then cold.

"Great," I say.

"I want you to walk behind me," Kara says. "From this point on. Just walk behind me, and don't talk to me unless I address you first."

Marta laughs. "Kara!"

"You heard Anna," Kara says. "We own her. Hurry the fuck up, Regina. We've waited long enough."

I grip the edges of the sink. "Give me a second."

"*Now.*"

I run the water as hard as it will go.

". . . Let her have her second," Kara finally mutters. They leave me at the sink. My second turns into a minute, and then another. The door opens again. Anna.

"You've had your *second*," she spits. I turn off the tap and we leave the washroom. Jeanette's there with the others. As the five of us make our way down the hall together, Anna leans over. "I'm so glad you chickened out this morning, Regina. A lunchtime entrance will be better. *Everyone* will see it."

It isn't until we're at the door to the cafeteria that I begin to register the people around us. They're whispering and pointing, and then I remember our outfits, totally completing this nightmare. I glance at the other girls and it's skirts and cardigans all the way down. I roll my shoulders and try to get the dirty feeling off me, but I can't.

I take a deep breath and enter the cafeteria with them.

It's not like everyone notices at once. There's no awed hush as we make our way to the center table. The room is buzzing the way it usually is, until the realization *Regina Afton is back in* hits the left side, and there's a subtle shift, the frequency changes, and makes its way back across the cafeteria. I feel lightheaded, and my neck is so tense when I turn my head to look at the Garbage Table, I'm afraid it'll snap.

Michael's oblivious. It hasn't reached him yet. I'm comforted by this, like it buys me time—for what, I don't know—

But then he looks up.

His eyes travel over Anna and Kara, and when they get to me, there's this flicker, something torn between recognition—*I know that girl*—and total incomprehension: *What is she doing over there?* Anna jostles me over to the center table, but I can't look away from him, until his mouth drops open and then I have to.

Josh, Henry, and Bruce are already at the table, dutifully waiting for us girls. It's so horribly familiar, I wander to the seat next to Josh, where I used to sit, before Anna pulls me back.

"Best friends should sit together," she says.

She takes my old seat and settles in next to Josh. His lunch tray is fixed up for two. He slides her half over and gives her a kiss on the cheek. Anna points to the seat between her and Bruce, and I sit down. Being this close to Bruce is disgusting and recalls the smell of the supply closet, which sends my gut into a somersault routine. I try to ignore it and take a slow look around the table. Josh's expression is unreadable, or he just doesn't care. Marta is picking at her fingernails, waiting for a cue from a higher-up. Jeanette is giving the straw in her juice box head, hoping Henry will notice. He does. Kara's oddly somber. I thought she'd enjoy this more. A lot more.

Anna unwraps a granola bar and looks at me. "Aren't you eating?"

"No."

"Eat."

"Anna, if you make me eat, I will puke all over you."

"Then at least smile. Let everyone know how happy you are to be here."

I force a smile at her and the right side of my mouth starts twitching. I feel Michael's eyes on me now the most. I really, really don't want to see his face.

"Well." Bruce leans back. "If you're not eating, Regina, I need a drink. I'm sure Kara and Marta could use one, too. Why don't you run up there and get us some Coke?"

"That'd be nice," Marta says. "On Regina."

"I don't have my wallet."

Bruce digs into his pocket and tosses a bill at me. "Get it, girl."

I stare at the money.

"Go," Anna says. "And don't forget to smile."

I grab the bill, push my chair out, and stand. I make the biggest, most painful close-mouthed smile I can muster, and then I'm in a long lineup. Smiling.

"What are you doing?"

My heart goes into overdrive. Michael. Right next to me in this line. I keep my eyes on the menu tacked to the wall, still smiling. I can't look at him or I'll give it away. If I give it away, he is fucked. So the only thing I can think to do is pretend that he's not here. I stare straight ahead.

"It's a joke, right?" The line moves up. "Regina."

"We had a good talk yesterday," I say. The line moves up again. I want it to go faster. I can feel the center table. All their eyes on me. "We're friends again."

"I don't believe you."

"She finally believed me about Donnie," I say distractedly. The line moves up again, and I rub the back of my neck. I blink once, twice, three times. *Don't cry, don't cry, don't cry.* "So it's okay."

"I don't believe you," he repeats. "Not after yesterday." I reach the cash register and ask for three Cokes. He keeps talking. "Why are you doing this? You're wearing the same outfits—"

The lunch lady hands me the drinks. I hand her the bill.

"Go away, Michael," I say.

Anna "rescues" me then. She wraps an arm around me, and I try to act like it's a welcome move by forcing my third smile of the day. At her.

"What's going on?"

"Nothing." I hand her one of the Cokes and shove the change in my pocket. "Come on, let's take these back."

"We're talking," Michael says.

"We're done."

"We're talking."

"No, we're not."

I push past him. Anna is on my heels, her voice in my ear:

"You didn't tell him, did you?"

"Does he look like I told him?"

"No," she says, glancing over her shoulder. "He actually looks pretty devastated."

At the end of the day, I know Michael's going to be waiting for me in his car. He'll trail me home and he'll try to get me to talk. I'm so desperate to avoid it, I ask Anna for a ride home and she laughs in my face, so I have to detour down the main street and then detour into Ford's, where I buy three packs of antacids.

Michael calls. It's the first time he's ever called. I don't answer. And then Anna calls and tells me yellow. Tomorrow we'll be wearing yellow.

I can't eat my dinner.

I skip breakfast and head to school, because I don't want to risk running into Michael. I stake out a spot at the front door and wait for the rest of the group to show, just like old times. It takes about thirty minutes. Kara's first to show. She stands next to me, quiet. I just want to kill her.

"Don't get comfortable," she says.

I turn to her. "What?"

"Don't get comfortable," she repeats slowly. "This was Anna's idea, but I'd rather see you dead after that e-mail than pretend we're friends for the rest of the year, no matter how miserable it makes you. I'm not done with you, so don't get comfortable."

It never stops.

"Don't tempt me, Kara."

"Watch your back, Regina."

"Go fuck yourself, Kara."

Jeanette and Marta bound up to us—to Kara—then. I put a little space between us. Waiting for Anna is hell on my stomach, and I've taken three antacids by the time she arrives, wearing one of the lowest cut tops I've ever seen. Marta whistles.

"I hope you don't plan on bending over today."

"Only in front of Josh," she replies, grinning.

Michael's car pulls into the parking lot before I can roll my eyes at what she's said. My stomach twinges. "Let's go in. Please."

Anna spots him. "No."

I watch him make his way toward the school. It doesn't really hurt yet, seeing him but not being near him. I think I'm still in shock. I hunch my shoulders and edge closer to Anna, like that'll make me invisible, but she notices and steps away from me.

When Michael reaches us, he keeps walking.

"He cannot have gotten over it that fast," Anna says, watching him go. "You didn't tell him, did you? Because if you did—"

"No! I didn't—I haven't talked to him at all. He called me last night and I didn't even pick up. I didn't tell him, Anna, I swear—"

"I know you didn't." She grins. "I just wanted to see you squirm."

"*Bitch.*"

Kara, Marta, and Jeanette gasp.

We're all wearing yellow.

I walk away. Anna calls me back. I keep walking. I'm shoving my hands into my pockets, popping two antacids. I stop on the second floor and lean against a row of lockers. They won't find me here for a couple of minutes. But Liz does. Liz finds me. When she walks into my line of vision, I groan.

"What were they offering?" she asks.

"Liz, go away," I say.

"Michael asked me if I knew anything," she says. "He thinks you have a reason. Like he really thinks that what you're doing right now *doesn't* make sense."

"Anna wanted to be friends again," I say. "I can spend the rest of my year getting locked in closets or I can be friends with *Michael*. And you should be happy. You didn't want me anywhere near him."

"You're a bitch," she says.

"Hey, self-preservation. Don't blame me because you and Michael were too stupid to figure it out and got hurt."

"This is so shocking," she says sarcastically. "But once a coward . . ."

I can't wait until I'm too dead inside to feel this. I leave her there. I make my way to my locker. Josh, Anna, and Henry are there, and all of a sudden I can't see. I can't see, I can't breathe. I turn before they see me. I'm halfway down the hall from them when the bell rings and I realize I need my books for class.

I head back to my locker, and they're still there. I shove Josh aside and fumble with my lock. I don't say a word. They don't say a word to me.

Because I just have to be a part of this scene. Not belong to it.

"Come on," Anna is saying, squeezing Josh's shoulder, nearly falling out of her top. Josh gets all disappointed when she doesn't. "One more party."

"I don't know. It's getting kind of cold out."

"That's what the bonfire's for," Henry says.

Josh punches him in the arm. "You just want to get wasted."

"I don't need an excuse," Henry replies. "But I *do* like getting wasted in a group setting." He belches. "I refuse to accept that last monstrosity of a party as *the* last party of the season."

"Seriously." Anna eyes me. "Come on, Josh. This weekend. You said—"

"Can't," Josh replies. "My dad's here this weekend, and I need to get some of his prescriptions and restock first. I mean, if you want it to be a really *good* party . . ."

The bell rings. They trail down the hall. When they're about twenty steps away from me, Anna notices I'm not trailing after them. She stops. Turns. Snaps her fingers. Points to the empty space beside her.

"Regina," she says. "Here."

My only solace is the weekend.

It comes.

And then it goes.

My YourSpace revenge is dead in the water. Anna's scheme works better than even she anticipated; the re-formation of the Fearsome Five-some distracts everyone for a second and settles too quickly. Every-one in this school has seen me stand beside Anna before.

It's new, but it's old.

Gym.

Nelson is dividing us into teams for basketball when I start feel-ing not right. I take an antacid before I realize it's not my stomach—it's my head. It doesn't feel attached to my neck, and then it does, and then I'm very aware of a slow-building pressure behind my eyes that threatens to become the kind of headache that will make me vomit—or would, if there was anything in my stomach to vomit up.

I raise my hand. Nelson points at me. "What it is, Afton?"

"Can I be excused?" I ask. "I don't feel well."

I wish I could take it back. The whole class hears it. That's Anna, that's Michael, that's Kara, that's Josh, that's Donnie. I don't want them looking at me, and now they are. Nelson studies me, and I must look bad because she doesn't run me through the usual twenty questions reserved for suspected fakers.

"Hayden," she says. Michael looks up. "Escort your friend to the nurse's office."

It's like someone dumped a bucket of ice down my shirt. Michael crosses the gym. My eyes meet Anna's. She gives me a warning look. And a smirk.

"So let's go," he says.

Nelson resumes splitting the class, and Michael and I make our way out. The throbbing in my head gets worse. When we hit the hall, I focus on the quiet and pray it stays, but it doesn't. Of course it doesn't. He wants answers.

"What do they have on you?"

I exhale slowly. I don't know whether to feel really good or bad that he doesn't believe I'd do that to him. It makes it harder, either way.

"They don't have anything on me," I say.

"You look like hell."

"Thanks."

He grabs me by the arm. "You were so happy to be rid of them and now you're *friends* again? Bullshit. What do they have on you?"

"I *said* they don't have anything on me—"

"They have to," he says, desperate. I can see the hurt building, and my stomach isn't having it. "You wouldn't be doing this to me if they didn't have something on you—"

"I—" I focus on the poster tacked to the wall behind his head. A bedraggled kitten is clinging to a tree branch. *Hang in there!* I can't think around my headache. "I told you. Anna found out that it was true about Donnie, that Kara lied, so she's—she felt terrible about it. So—we're friends again."

"You can barely *lie*," he says. I start protesting halfheartedly, because I really don't feel well. It makes it easy for him to talk over me. "If that's the truth, then what about Kara? Anna wouldn't let Kara get away with that."

Goddammit. If he were Jeanette or Marta he would've bought it by now. I'm not making friends with people who are smart, from this point on. Ever again.

"Tell me," he begs.

"I told you. We're friends again. I told Liz—"

"You didn't mean what you said to Liz."

"It doesn't *matter*, Michael," I burst out. "Because whatever it is, even after everything between us, I still weighed it—them or you—and I didn't choose you. I knew how hard it was for you to choose me, and I *still picked them*. I mean, that's basically picking their bullshit over you, right? I didn't choose you, and I totally wasted your time, so even if they *do* have something on me, *it doesn't matter*."

It's a hit. Finally. He flinches like I've slapped him and takes a step back.

"I put myself out there for you," he says slowly. "I can't believe I—"

"I needed someone to put between me and Anna, and you probably never even really liked me." I dig the knife further in, but I'm not sure I need to. "You were really lonely, and I was there after a long time of no one being there."

He takes another step back. "You—"

I wish he would shout at me. He doesn't. This quiet devastation creeps across his face and he fights it, and it reminds me of that day in the diner, and I feel like my heart is breaking. But it's still not as bad as what Anna will do to him if I tell him the truth.

"I should have known," he finally says, and I wince because he was the best thing that ever happened to me. He takes another step back. "Easy way out, every single time. Liz told me—*fuck*—I can't believe I let you do this to me *twice*."

I can't wait for him to go, so I go.

By the time I reach the washroom, my head is killing me, and the disgusting fluorescent lights overhead makes it feel worse. I gag over the sink, but nothing comes out. I lean forward and take deep, even breaths in and out, and then I run the water as cold as it will go, cupping my hands together for a drink. It doesn't help. I wet a paper towel, sit on the floor—gross—and press it against my eyes.

After a while, the paper towel loses its chill, but I can't find the will to get up and wet it again. Michael hates me. He hates me. I start to cry, keeping the paper towel against my eyes and letting it soak up my tears. When the door swings open, I can't inspire myself to care. Getting up and trying to act okay is so beyond me right now.

"Oh, Regina."

Anna's voice is motherly. Awful. I keep the towel against my eyes. She crosses the room and sits beside me. She presses something crumbly and dry into my hands. I look down. An oatmeal cookie. I blink and take in the room. Anna's beside me. Kara's leaning against the door, ensuring no one will come in.

I don't care if Anna sees me cry, but Kara . . .

I wipe at my eyes with my free hand.

"Eat," Anna urges me. I shake my head. She grabs me by the chin and makes me look at her. "Come on. I don't make you *that* sick. Eat or else."

That whole year she thought I was starving myself—after Kara actually *did* starve herself—she used that voice. *Eat.* I take a bite of the cookie and revive a little at the food in my mouth. My stomach doesn't want it. I clamp my hand over my mouth.

It takes forever to swallow.

"Kara, wait outside," Anna says, when I finally do.

"What? No way. I want to see this."

"Wait outside *now.*"

Kara knows better than to argue. She yanks the door open and steps into the hall.

"Talk to Michael?" Anna asks me. I nod. "Did it hurt?"

The last three words set me off. My face crumples and I bring my knees up to my chest, burying my face in them.

"So now you know exactly how I felt when I found out you slept with Donnie."

"Jesus *Christ*, Anna. I didn't fucking sleep with Donnie. He tried to—"

"Don't. *Shut. Up.* Listen to me: All that time I thought you were my best friend," she says. "You were like a sister to me. Now, thanks to Michael's journal, I find out I just made you sick. This will *never*

get better for you, okay? I want you to understand what you ruined
and how good you had it." She tucks an errant strand of hair behind
my ear. I jerk away. "And then . . . I want you to be sorry."

"I'm sorry," I tell her desperately. "Anna, *I'm sorry.*"

"No, you're not," she says. "I'll let you know."

"Look at this," Anna says as Jeanette, Marta, and Kara cluster around her. We've finished gym. Fresh out of the showers and in the changing rooms. Anna is holding up a thin silver chain with a silver pendant dangling off it. "Just because. That's what he said."

It's like partying all night with people you hate and bypassing home to go straight to your job so you can work all day with more people you hate.

And never stopping.

"Ooh, my God," Jeanette says softly, cupping it in her palm. Anna grins, beside herself with squeally-girl joy. "You know what that means, right? Sex."

And it does, too. I have something similar abandoned in a jewelry box at home. And the five of us talked about what that meant when Josh gave it to me then. This is a special kind of hell—listening to my ex–best friend wax about fucking my ex-boyfriend. I get dressed as slowly as possible so I can avoid walking down the hall with them, but it's a give-and-take. I have to listen to this stupid babbling until they go.

I stare at Anna until she notices and sets the necklace back against her neck. I can't resist: "Doesn't it bother you at all that whatever you do with Josh, I did first?"

"Anything you do, I do better."

"There's a learning curve," I tell her.

"Go to hell."

"Oh, I'm there."

"Speaking of hell," Marta interjects, "has anyone seen Donnie lately? He's lost like, twenty pounds. He looks like a piece of shit."

"He must be good enough for you now, Kara," I say, pulling on my pants. "Maybe he's desperate enough to have you."

"I wouldn't touch your castoffs with a thirty-foot pole," she snaps. "I have some standards."

There's always something amazing about watching people fuck themselves over. We all realize what Kara's said at the exact same moment. Anna's jaw drops, and Kara's face goes from peach to pale in two seconds flat. If I could guarantee she did something this stupid every day, getting up in the morning would be infinitely easier.

"*What* did you say?"

Kara spews apologies. They dribble from her mouth and fall on deaf ears.

"Anna, I'm sorry—I am so, so sorry. I didn't mean it like that. I'm sorry—"

"Because Josh is Regina's castoff, isn't he, so—"

"I'm *sorry*! That was at Regina, it wasn't at you—"

"Fuck off, Kara."

Silence. This is the kind of silence that used to make me so uncomfortable and queasy to be in the middle of and grateful to not be on the receiving end of.

I like it today.

The rest of the girls get dressed quietly and leave when the bell rings. I pull my shirt on and then I leave, too. As soon as I step into the busy halls, I feel weight, pressure. My chest tightens and it's, like—grief. Everywhere.

I pull the collar of my shirt into my mouth and bite and try to get through the moment. I don't know that I *can* get through this moment.

I need to see who I'm doing this for.

I stake out Michael's locker. He's been avoiding me and hanging out with Liz, which makes sense. I've only glimpsed him in the halls, and I can't stare at him at lunch too long because Anna gets off on it when I do, and I'm afraid he'll look back and I will finally break. After a couple minutes, he shows. He looks as unaffected as he always does, and I try to talk myself out of this loss, but I can't. I hope he's angry. I hope he hates me, because then he can have that and it'll carry him through.

"That's really obvious," a voice says beside me.

I close my eyes briefly. "Go away, Josh."

"Anna told me to tell you." He points down the hall, where Anna's with Bruce and Kara and Marta and Jeanette. She smiles and waves. "You're being really obvious."

Michael looks up and spots us both. I swallow down the bile making its way up my throat and turn to Josh. "Nice necklace you gave Anna. I totally still have mine. That means sex, right?"

Josh scratches the back of his neck. "And I'm totally not comfortable having this conversation with my ex-girlfriend. And why the hell should you care? At least I waited until *after* we broke up before I decided to screw other people."

"Fuck you."

"Anyway, the lady beckons." He takes me by the arm and forces me down the hall, smiling at Anna as we approach. As soon as he's close enough, he moves away from me, wraps his arm around her, and gives her a light kiss on the lips. Barf.

"Dad's-out-of-town-Thursday," he says, kissing her between words. She's putty in his hands. "I've restocked. It's short notice and I'd rather it be a weekend, but this is our only chance, and the weather's supposed to be good, so . . . party. My house."

"I like the way you think." She grins.

Josh turns to the hall, projecting his voice and silencing the idle chatter around us. "Party at my house Thursday. Got that?" He points to a pair of juniors. "Get the word out. Last one this season." He turns back to Anna and kisses her on the nose. "You will be there, of course."

"Of course." She giggles. He smiles and marches down the hall, the boys trailing after him. They stop to tell anyone who's someone about the party.

Anna turns to us, and she has this stupid, stupid look on her face. "Oh, my God, I can't wait." And then it's like, this group squeal that I don't take part of. She notices this and takes offense. "Oh, and Regina? You're coming. Designated driver."

Kara snickers. "Try not to get almost raped this time, okay?"

*Die.* They laugh. The bell rings. We make our way down the hall, jostling through the crowd until we reach the top of the stairs. *She has to die.*

"Watch it," Kara says, jamming her elbow into my side.

I don't even think about it: My foot slips in front of hers, sending her tumbling down the stairs. A shocked noise passes my lips. I can't believe I did it, but I'm glad I did, until her fall is interrupted by a group of stair-loitering freshman. I stand at the top of the stairs and watch Anna, Marta, and Jeanette rush to her. I read Kara's lips: *I'm fine, I'm fine.* She shrugs them off and looks my way. She knows.

"I hope it's worth it."

I turn. Michael. And the way he says it is so damning, so disgusted.

"It's worth it," I whisper.

It's for him. He shakes his head and walks away. I force myself down the stairs and past Anna and everyone while they're distracted. I don't feel like going straight to an empty house, so I wander around town for a while.

Almost every place in Hallowell is the same kind of unremarkable, except for Josh's place. I stay away from that side of town and turn onto Hainsworth. Jeanette lives here. Donnie. I can see his home from here. It's all gray siding with a weak garden out front, but every little bit of it is immaculately kept.

And his black convertible is in the center of it all.

He found it.

I take a quick look around. The place looks empty. I approach the house, his car, and I take it all in. It should be fantastic. I should love the ugly lines I made down his convertible. I should love that everyone else can see them, too. I should love that there's a crack down the windshield that wasn't there before. I don't.

It makes me miss Michael.

I circle the car, and when I return to the scratches, I reach out. I want to see what that kind of damage feels like. I press my fingers against the metal body.

The front door bursts open.

"Get the fuck away from my car."

"I told you it'd turn up," I say.

Donnie stands there, raging on the steps. I edge over to the front of the car and bring my hand to the windshield. Baiting him should feel good. It doesn't.

"Get away from my car," he repeats. I run my hand over the fresh crack on the windshield. "Stop it."

I trace the line in the glass down to the windshield wipers.

"*Stop*—"

"Oh, sorry, *you* want *me* to *stop*? Hey, tell Anna. Go and tell Anna that you tried to rape me. Tell her."

His mouth hangs open, like he can't decide to step forward or back into the house, and I hate the silence, so I kick the convertible as hard as I can.

"*Afton*—"

"That's what you get, Donnie." I kick it again. "For what you did to me."

He turns purple-faced and makes his way over to me. A car rolls down the street, slowing as it passes. I take the opportunity to move out, and when I glance back, he's heading back inside his house, slamming the door shut behind him.

I glance at the clock on my nightstand. Eight-thirty. Probably everyone is well on their way to wasted. Designated driver.

Boring.

I used to really hate the last party of the season, even if I drank until I was blind. They were always bigger. Louder. More drinks, dancing, drugs, fucking, more fucking around. Last year, Henry totaled his car while driving home. He broke his collarbone.

I change into a black hoodie and jeans—incognito. Running into Anna is inevitable, but I don't have to make it easy for her to spot me.

"I think it's nice," Mom says as I make my way to the door. I stop and turn to her. She smiles. "That you and Josh can still be friends. Have fun at the party."

"Yeah," I say.

When I reach Josh's house, instant sensory overload. Too many sights, sounds, and smells. It's chilly out, but all the bodies give the illusion of warmth. I pass these crazy girls dancing on the front lawn. They're in the moment, and the moment is them, and the moment is perfect. The party is here and it's perfect. Music. Cars. Friends.

I'm not feeling it.

I step into the heart of the scene, and in a minute flat, a bottle of beer is pressed into my hand by some kid who doesn't know I'm the designated driver. It's tempting, but I leave it unopened. I have a headache. Already. I cross my arms and stay on the lawn, bored. After a while, Anna, Kara, and Jeanette march up.

"Anyone need a ride home?" I ask.

"Party's barely started," Anna says. "We're not over it yet."

"Where's Marta? Is she over it yet?"

"Strip Monopoly," Kara says.

"Hey—" Jeanette stumbles forward and relieves me of my beer. "You can't have this. You're the designated driver." She cracks it open and pounds it. For a second, I envy her. "This is the best party ever."

Anna rips the bottle from her hands. "Jesus, Jeanette. It's too early for you to be this wasted. If Regina has to drive you home before midnight, I'll kick your ass."

"Why?" I ask her. "That's what I'm here for."

"Yeah, but you don't want to be here." Anna takes a sip of the stolen beer. "So I want to keep you here as long as possible."

Jeanette reaches for the bottle. "Give. Get your own."

"Kara, get me a beer out of the cooler," Anna says.

"But it's around the other side of the house," Kara whines.

"I don't care. Get me one."

She goes. It's pathetic how she goes.

"Nailed Josh yet?" I ask Anna.

"Later," she says. "Do you think I should go back there?"

I shrug. "I don't give a damn."

She sighs. "Do you think he'd think I was needy? I didn't call him today or anything. If I went back there, do you think he'd mind? I don't want to be overbearing."

"*You* don't want to be overbearing?" God, I wish I had a drink. "That's funny."

"You should maybe *try* to get on my good side," she snaps. "It doesn't have to be *totally* miserable for you all the time."

"It's never been anything but, Anna." I study her. "So you really like him, huh?"

Of course she likes him. And the question throws her off, like

I want it to. She opens her mouth and flushes, and it's these small things, these gives that Anna works hard to keep off her face that could be her downfall if anyone just looked closely enough.

But I was the only one who did.

"Why?" she asks. "Going to steal him back?"

"Oh, yeah," I say. "Watch out."

She gives me a look like she can't stand being around me, and then she goes, which is totally great. I watch a group of sophomores force a poor frosh to take an impossible sip from a bottle of rye. Jeanette sucks on the beer. After a while, Kara returns with the one Anna sent her for.

"Where the hell did Anna go?" she demands.

I shrug.

"Did she say where she was going?"

"I think she forgot about you."

"Fuck off, Regina."

I cross my arms and stare up at the sky. No stars. Nothing.

"I'm still not sorry, Kara," I tell her.

"And that's exactly why you're there," she says. "And I'm here now."

"Right. Enjoy your moment. Doesn't that bother you? You'll probably go your whole life and it won't be this good again. You've totally peaked."

She stares at me. "What if it's your moment?"

"This isn't my moment," I tell her. "This is my penance."

"For what? For Liz? For Michael?"

I bite the inside of my cheek. "Shut up."

"Isn't it funny how you tried to get back in good with Michael and Liz, and it didn't work? I think that means if this is your penance for anything," she says, "it's your penance for what you did to me, and it will be until you're sorry."

"You think I'd give you that? After all this?"

Her face turns red. "You didn't even have a good reason. You didn't even have one single good reason to treat me the way you did."

"I didn't know I needed one of those."

I leave her there. My stomach aches, aches, aches, and this is stupid. It's stupid because I'm worried what Kara said is true. This is what I get until I pay up, but how can I have gone through everything I've gone through and still not be paid up? *Sorry, sorry, sorry.* I never want to apologize to her. Ever. I hate that idea. Hate it. I make my way around the house and find Josh lurking beneath a tree in the backyard away from the party and the bonfire. Anna-less. He's nursing a bottle of Jack Daniels. He takes a swig and I try to pass him unnoticed, but he grabs my arm.

"Regina, wait—"

I pull away from him. "You can't possibly need a ride home."

He doesn't say anything. We stare at each other. It's weird. I move to leave again, but he grabs me by the arm again. His hand stays on me this time.

"What's wrong with you?" I ask.

He takes a long pull from the bottle. The party sounds fill the air. He shakes his head and bites his index finger before speaking. "Regina, I'm sorry I didn't—"

"Shut up." I step back, my heart sinking to my stomach. "Who told you—"

"Anna was laughing about it with Kara," he says. "She said you said he tried to rape you." He looks away from me. "That's what you wanted to tell me that night—"

"Yeah, I know. I was there."

"Fuck. I mean—*fuck.*" He takes another swig of the Jack. "I can't fucking believe this. *Fuck.* I am so—"

"Choke on it, Josh."

He flinches. "Seriously—don't. Like—" He twitches, like he can't stand himself, and I'm glad, that makes me happy because he should know that feeling at least once. "I can't stop thinking about it. It changes everything—it totally—"

"Are you going to tell Anna it's the truth?" I ask. He looks away. No. He's not. "Then it doesn't change anything."

He closes his eyes and leans back against the tree. This is what I wanted this whole time, and it doesn't change anything. No one will ever benefit from knowing this. It's now completely worthless information, designed to make people feel bad.

It still happened and it was horrible. But it's worthless.

I am so empty.

"I'm sorry," he repeats.

"Got any Percocet? Or just Adderall?"

"I've got everything." He takes another swig from the bottle and stares at me. I stare back at him expectantly. "Are you serious?" he says. "You want Percocet?"

"Yes."

"It'll really fuck you up. It's not like you take them every day—"

"One night, Josh. If you're sorry, you'll give it to me."

How can he refuse? He takes another drink, grabs my hand, and leads me around the edge of the house, unseen. We go upstairs, to his room. He digs into his sock drawer, and a second later I have the pills. Plural. He must feel *really* bad.

He must think they'll help.

"On the house," he says. "Unless you want to pay me."

"No."

"Peace offering?"

"Sure." Like hell.

"Regina, I'm really sorry—"

"Shut the fuck up," I say tiredly.

I leave him in his bedroom and head to the bathroom, where I sit on the edge of the tub and stare at the Percocet. Is this what it was like for Liz? Trying to find a decent ending for herself in a bunch of pills? But I don't want to die.

I just don't want to be here. I never wanted to be here.

I'm not sure I've ever been here.

There's something automatic and familiar about the Percocet. I didn't do pills at parties before. I just drank. Because it made it easier to be here, but—

I catch sight of myself in the mirror. There are bags under my eyes and my face is pale and the corners of my mouth are edging down of their own accord. The pills feel heavy in my palm, as heavy as Donnie's keys in my palm. But that was different.

I curl my fingers around the pills and close my eyes. I want them. One. That's how I do these things. *Coward.* Liz is right. Coward. I want to be better than that someday. If it's possible. Is it possible. I hope. . . .

I open my hand. I flush them down the toilet.

I stay in the bathroom for an hour and then I decide I'm leaving and I'm not driving anyone home.

I'm making my way out of the house when some sophomore corners me and tells me Bruce is looking for me because he needs a ride. I groan and modify my plans, because I don't want him to get in a car if he's totally plastered. I have to make him someone else's problem. I leave the house and make my way to the backyard, to the bonfire. Henry's lounging in a chair.

"Is Josh here?" I ask him.

Henry shrugs. "He was."

My eyes travel to an empty bottle of vodka lying on the ground.

"Henry," I say.

"He's inside," he says, closing his eyes. And then a warning: "Anna's probably close."

I go back inside and climb up the stairs. Maybe he's in his bedroom, but I hope not. If he's there, Anna's with him. I don't want to see them fucking.

Josh's bedroom door is open. No one's inside. I make my way back down the stairs, and a sliver of light filtering across the floor from inside the den catches my eye.

My last memories of the den aren't good.

But Donnie's not there.

I push the door open. Josh is sprawled on the couch, his right leg dangling off the side, his arm thrown haphazardly across his eyes. I cross the room and stand over him, and his glassy eyes take me in.

As soon as he registers my face, he struggles into a sitting position and pats the space next to him. I sit down.

He rubs his eyes. "Is Anna back?"

"Where did she go?"

"She drove Jeanette home because she couldn't find you. She's very, very mad about that. . . ."

Good. "I'm going home. Tell Anna I went." Josh brings his hand up to my face. I brush it away. "Don't touch me."

His face falls, devastated, like it's some leftover from what happened with Donnie, even though it's more that I still hate Josh. He edges closer to me and says pathetically, "I'm really sorry, Regina."

"Josh, don't—"

It doesn't stop him. He wraps his arms around me, like that's *sorry*. Like it makes everything right, even though it's so far from ever being right again. He tightens his grip on me, like he's trying to get his apology into my bones, but it'll never work. And then he pulls away a little and holds my face in his hand and brings his mouth really close to mine. At first, I think he's going to kiss me, but he doesn't. He keeps his mouth close so he can apologize into mine. I can smell the booze on his breath.

"I'm so sorry," he says, resting his forehead against mine. "I'm so sorry. . . ."

"What's going on?"

Josh lowers his hands. I turn slowly. Kara's voice is soft and interested.

"Nothing," I say. "I'm going home."

She looks me over. "What? Goddammit, you're the fucking *designated driver*, Regina. Who's going to drive Bruce home?"

I shrug. "You look pretty sober to me."

And then she starts spluttering and I go home.

# friday

The plan: Get to school before everyone else and hide out in the library, because I'm not looking forward to Anna today. She'll give me hell for bailing.

I leave the house while my parents are still asleep. The air is crisp. Each breath in stings a little, but it's sort of invigorating. A miniscule nice moment in a sea of feeling bad. I try to figure out a way I can hold on to that. I'm holding on to it until Anna's Benz pulls up beside me, and then my moment goes away.

"Kara totally said you'd try to get there before us," Anna says, leaning over Kara, who is in the passenger's side. Marta and Jeanette are in the back. "Get in."

"I'll walk."

"Regina, it's too early in the morning to threaten you with black-mail. Get in."

I sigh. Marta gets out of the car and waits for me to crawl in. As soon as we're all wedged side by side in the back, Anna U-turns. We're headed away from the school.

"Where are we going?" I ask.

"Breakfast. I'm not going in this early."

I pop an antacid and rest my head against the seat, and they get fast food from the local strip. The car fills with that fatty, greasy smell and I try to tune out the chewing and talking, but it's impossible. I keep waiting for Anna to bitch me out for failing my duties last

night, but it never happens, so I let myself relax a little and watch
the road disappear under the space of windshield visible between
her and Kara.

"So good," Jeanette says, popping the last of a greasy breakfast
muffin into her mouth. "I'm so fucking hungover. I thought I was
going to *die* last night."

"I told you to pace yourself." Anna turns on the radio, settling
on a station that will please her and none of us. "That reminds me.
Thanks for fucking us over, Regina."

There it is. "You didn't really think I'd stay, did you?"

She doesn't say anything. I reach into my pocket for another antacid. Houses blur past the window. Anna drives aimlessly and turns
the car onto a deserted stretch of road. I check the clock. We're going to be late.

"We'll be late if you don't turn around now," I tell her.

"Who cares? It's Friday. Besides, I know you can't stand being
around us, so I'm just prolonging your torture," Anna says. "That's
worth being late for."

I close my eyes and they start blathering—going over the finer
points of the party like they're worth going over—while I focus on
the radio. I don't even notice the car roll onto the shoulder until the
keys jangle out of the ignition and kill the song that's playing.

We've stopped.

All four doors open. I open my eyes. Jeanette and Marta get out
of the car first, followed by Kara and Anna. I'm in the backseat
totally alone.

Okay.

"Get out." Kara. "Get out of the car, Regina."

The words come out honey-slow, oozing off her lips and into my
ears. All at once, I understand what's happening. Drop and ditch.
Bruce planted it into Anna's head when she was brainstorming ways
to make Liz miserable, and I somehow managed to convince her it
wasn't "cerebral" enough. She really wanted to do it, though.

And now she can.

I leave the car slowly, all too aware of how cold it is now that I know I'm going to be stuck out here. I gauge the distance. Hallowell is a long walk back.

"I didn't see this coming," I admit.

"That was the idea," Anna replies, standing behind Kara and looking strangely second in command. "Give Kara your shoes."

Jeanette and Marta stand behind me like stone walls. Kara grins and holds out her hands, looking like she's got all the time in the world. In the grand scheme of things, this isn't that bad. It's not the WHORE spray-painted on my locker or another YourSpace page, and it's not being locked in a closet with Donnie Henderson. It's not losing Michael again. It's a long walk in sock feet when it's cold outside. It's a long walk in sock feet when it's cold outside without *them*.

So that's practically a vacation.

I crouch down, fumble with my shoes, take them off, and hand them over. My socks are thin and the ground is colder than the air. My toes curl in. Kara throws my shoes into the back of the car, yanks my book bag out, and tosses it onto the road.

"Okay," she says.

Marta and Jeanette grab my arms and force them behind my back. I try to jerk away before I really understand it, but they hold tight.

"What—?"

"You really fucked up this time, Regina," Kara sings.

"Jesus, are you kidding me? Because I decided I didn't want to drive you guys home?"

"No, it's more like because you were all over Josh in the den last night," Anna says. "Kara told me she saw you together."

My jaw drops. Kara grins, daring me to deny it.

"I don't get it, Regina. Did you just give up? A final 'fuck you'? You knew how I felt about—" She crosses her arms. "You knew."

"Yeah," I say, resigned. "I knew."

"Is that all you have to say?"

I nod. Kara nudges Anna, who takes a few uncertain steps forward.

Kara nods at her encouragingly and says, "Just don't forget to tuck your thumb in, okay? In."

Anna nods and brings her arm back.

Oh, wait.

"Anna, Anna, Anna—Anna, don't—"

Her fist connects awkwardly with my jaw, because Anna's never punched anyone before. She doesn't know how. Still, I've been punched. My knees give a little at the shock of it, but Marta and Jeanette keep me upright. It's dead silence and then—

Anna starts to laugh.

"Shit!" she cries, clutching her hand. An achy warmth spreads across my jaw. No, not warmth. *Pain.* "Shit, you guys—that kind of hurt! *Shit.*"

Marta and Jeanette laugh with her. Kara grabs Anna's hand and runs her thumb over it, smiling. Anna keeps giggling, lost to the thrill of punching me in the face.

"You're okay," Kara tells her. "Want to go again?"

Marta and Jeanette tighten their grip on my arms. They want her to. I can feel it. Anna rubs her wrists, chuckling, until she looks at me. My heart stops while she sizes me up. I don't want her to go again. She can only get better at this.

"No," she finally says.

"Oh, come on," Kara says. "We've got her. We can fuck her up. You can't just bring her out this far and punch her *once.*"

"Fuck off, Kara," I say.

Kara turns to me. "What did you say?"

"I said 'Fuck off.'"

She walks over. "You know you have your arms held behind your back, right?"

"You know you'll never have this chance again," I say. "Right?"

She doesn't even prep. She draws her arm back and her fist connects with my stomach, and she hits harder than Anna. I can *see* the hit. It's in front of me—light, everywhere. If Jeanette and Marta weren't holding me up, I'm sure I'd be on my ass. The lights fade and the scene comes back. Before I can get a handle on it, Kara drives her fist into my stomach again and I crumple, my eyes watering. Jeanette and Marta drop me, because even they aren't expecting that second hit.

I can't breathe. I put my hand to the pavement. *Get up.* Kara's foot connects with my abdomen. My insides explode, and then it happens again: She kicks me again. I gag. Anna makes noise somewhere nearby. Jeanette and Marta move away. Kara's foot goes for my shoulder, and my brain sends frantic messages to my body saying *Get up, move,* so I roll onto my side and cover my head, leaving my back exposed, which is exactly where she gets me next. Hard. I roll onto my back, gasping, drowning. Kara kneels over me and covers my face with her hand, presses her palm over my mouth, my nose.

Our eyes meet.

There's nothing between us.

Nothing.

I claw at her arms, digging my nails into the bits of flesh her sweater doesn't cover. She winces and her hand is off my mouth. The air is razor sharp. I've barely tasted it when she grabs me by the shoulders and forces me into the ground. My head hits the road. The ocean is in my ears.

My hands drop.

Kara straightens and gets one last kick in. My side. I go in on myself and the adrenaline leaves me again and again and again, leaves me with this unbearable clarity where I know my feet are cold and my body is screaming and I can't move.

"You were just going to waste it," Kara yells at Anna. "You were just going to fucking waste it! *That's* what we came out here for!"

"Jesus, Kara," Jeanette breathes. "Have you lost your *mind*?"

"No, I'm good." She shakes her hand, glaring at me. "I'm good now."

I listen to the gravel-crunch of footsteps making their way back to the car, car doors opening and closing shut, and then quiet, and I'm alone.

"Get up."

I'm not alone.

"Regina, get up." *No.* Anna's breathing heavily, charged from the electricity of this. "Regina, *get up.*"

I don't say anything.

"I just want to know why," she says.

I roll onto my back and lick my lips. Dirty gray clouds move across the sky, white sunlight filtering in through the breaks. And the sky looks so *great* from here, I start to laugh. It hurts, but I do it anyway.

I laugh so hard I cry.

"Kara got you *again.*"

"She didn't."

"She *did*," I say, laughing. "She totally did. She got you again—"

"She didn't—"

"*Yes—*"

*"Kara's not that smart."*

It comes out of her mouth so vehemently, but so sincerely, I finally understand why I never, ever had a chance.

"You're so *stupid*, Anna."

She moves her foot like she's going to kick me like Kara's kicked me, and the laughter dies instantly. I raise my hands and cover my face. Nothing happens. She savors this victory in quiet, until the car starts up and the horn blares.

"Well, it's been really interesting, but I've got to go," she says. "You know. Get destroying your boyfriend underway. Monday's going to be great. Have a nice walk."

Michael. She gets in the car and they head down the road. *Michael.* I curl into the ground until I can feel it's cold everywhere and I know I have to move. I push myself up on my elbows, my knees. *Stand. Stand, Regina. It's easy. Stand.*

*You do it every day.*

I walk the entire way back to Hallowell on feet so cold I don't even notice when they step through broken glass, until my sock starts sticking to my heel and gravel starts sticking to my sock and I look down and there's blood. I don't know how long it takes me to get into town, but every second settles into my screaming bones. My stomach aches. My back aches. My jaw aches. My feet are numb.

All I can think is *Michael.*

*Michael. Michael. Michael.* The thought of him drags me to Hallowell, drags me down the back streets, past my empty house, and all the way to the school, because I have to tell him. He has to know what's coming.

I limp across the parking lot and yank the front doors open. I step inside. The place is quiet. Distant class noises float down the hall—the illusion of another ordinary day. The warm air levels me, makes me feel instantly stupid-headed and dull.

My stomach lurches.

I'm going to be sick.

I fumble down the hall, keeping one hand against the wall and the other over my mouth, trying to make my way unobtrusively to the girls' room. I know I can't be seen.

After forever, the pale blue door reveals itself. I pull it open and stumble in.

Charie Andrews is standing at the mirrors, fussing with her hair.

She stops when she sees me. Her eyes go wide as saucers. I lean against the door and close my eyes for a minute.

When I open them, she's looking at my feet. I breathe in and walk stiffly over to the sink. I tell myself there's nothing here to look at. The smell of the soap makes me even more nauseous, and she's barely stepped away from me when I throw up—nothing.

"Jesus," she mutters. I spit and then I rest my palms on the sink and try to get my bearings. I end up with my forehead against the mirror, staring down the drain, vaguely realizing this is not acting like there's nothing to look at.

Get it together, Regina.

I take one deep breath and then another. On the walk back, I could do this. I could see myself doing this, but now I think maybe I need to sit down.

I sit on the floor, my back against the wall, and close my eyes, waiting for every broken part of me to piece itself together enough to tell Michael what's coming, and I feel Charie's eyes on me that whole time, and I don't even have the energy to tell her to go to hell. And then the washroom door swings shut and she's gone.

My toes are thawing, prickling uncomfortably. I open my eyes. I need to wedge the garbage can under the door so no one can come and see me like this. No one else. I press my palms against the floor and try to get to my feet and—

I can't.

I move and every kicked part of me protests, so I wrap my arms around myself and listen to the slow, steady sound of the faucet dripping water into the sink, and it goes deep. For a second, I'm in my bed again. This morning hasn't started.

Everything is . . . fine.

The washroom door flies open. My heart stops and my head jerks up. When my eyes focus on the halo of blond hair set around a pale face, I just—Liz. Always here. No matter what I do, she's always going to be here. This suicide blonde, haunting me for the rest of my life, following me from one awful moment to the next.

"Oh, my God," she says. "Charie said you—"

She stops. We stare at each other, but I can't hold her gaze, and I feel her looking at me long after I look away. I lean my head against the wall and close my eyes.

"*Regina,*" Liz says sharply, like I'm dying right in front of her. I open my eyes and laugh a little at that thought. I realize I'm not cold anymore, I'm warm. Hot. My shirt is clinging to every bit of skin there is to cling to. My hair is stuck to my neck and my face.

"Go away," I say. Wait. No. I need her. *Take it back.* "Get Michael for me. I need to tell him something—"

"He doesn't want to talk to you," she says.

"Liz, please—"

"No."

Frustrated tears spring to my eyes. "Fuck you, Liz. You don't even *know*—"

"You got your ass kicked," she says, "*finally*, and you want Michael to come pick up the pieces. I know what they did to you. I was in that stall—" She points. "And Anna and Jeanette came in here giggling about it. I knew you were out on that road."

I stare at the floor. Tears spill out onto my cheeks. I wipe my eyes.

"God, Regina, I don't understand you. This is the *only thing* that could have happened. You think you're making easy choices, and every single time you have a good thing, you ruin it. Because you're a coward. *Don't* expect me to feel sorry for you."

"It's not like you wanted me to have it," I snap. She snorts. I grab the edges of the counter and try to get myself up but I can't. And I can feel how pathetic it is and I know how pathetic it looks. I can't get up and she's just standing there. I slam my palm against the floor. "Why are you even here if you're not going to *help*?"

Her mouth drops open. She looks away from me, ashamed. I've never seen that on her face before, and I don't even know how I managed it, until she says, "I wanted to see it."

It's such a bitch thing to say.

But I get it.

"Okay," I mumble. I don't care anymore. I grab the counter a second time and finally manage to get to my feet. I lean on it. My mouth is dry, parched. I run the water cold and dab it on my face. It makes me painfully, painfully awake. "If you feel like it, tell Michael not to—tell him not to come to school on Monday."

"What? Why?"

"You tell me. You know everything."

I take a hard step on my right foot, the one with the cut, and wince. I just want to get past Liz, out of the washroom, go home, and die. She grabs my arm.

"I'm not telling him anything if you don't tell me why."

I bite my lip. This is not about me and Liz. Michael.

"They have his journal," I tell her.

"*What?* Michael has his journal. I've seen it."

I shake my head. "They stole it. Anna made photocopies and returned it before he knew it was missing. She's going to plaster it over school."

She stares at me. "He has his journal, Regina."

"I saw the pages." My voice cracks. "I'm not telling you what they said. But there was something in there that could get him expelled—"

"I don't believe you."

"I don't care if you believe me."

"You could be lying just to—just to get me to feel sorry for—"

"He wrote that he wanted to *kill everyone in school*," I blurt out. Liz's eyes widen. "They're going to give it to Holt and say it's a death threat. Do you know what that could do to him? *I* don't lose anything if you don't tell him."

I push past her bony frame. The space between the stalls and the sinks is too narrow, and the corner of the counter rams into my kicked side. I make a dying-kitten kind of sound and curl in, one hand on my side, the other on the counter.

"Regina—"

"Just look." I manage. "You wanted to see it." I leave the wash-room and make my way down the empty hall. The bell rings at the exact same time I push back through the front door. My toes cringe at the reintroduction to the cold pavement. But this is nothing.

Nothing.

I climb the stairs to my bedroom and study my reflection in the full-length mirror mounted on my closet. My jaw is tender to touch, but I think it's going to be okay, because Anna can't hit. But Kara can. I lift my shirt so I can see the damage. There are already bruises forming, abstract works of art across my abdomen and what I can glimpse of my back.

I raid the mirrored cabinet over the sink in the bathroom. My fingers travel over antacids and prescriptions until I find the Tylenol with Codeine and I take three of those, and then I crawl into bed.

Everything hurts.

**I don't want to go to school today.**

I get dressed slowly, but I don't want to look at myself. I don't want to see it on me.

Bruises always look the worst when they're healing.

I pull the edges of my sweater down and grab the bottle of Tylenol on my desk. I shake two pills into my palm. I probably don't need them. It doesn't even hurt like it did. Not totally. I take them anyway.

Mom and Dad drink their coffee at the kitchen table. Get ready for work. I stay at the kitchen sink, quiet, staring out the window. It's cold out. It looks cold out.

Anna's probably already taken care of it.

I wonder if it will be big.

I hope he's not there.

I turn away from the window and grab my book bag.

"Be careful in gym," Dad says, nodding at the bruise on my chin. He smiles a little. "Next time *dodge* the ball, huh?"

I nod. Mom looks up from her coffee.

"Going in already?" she asks. I nod again because I can't speak. She gives me a thumbs-up. "That's great. Have a good day, honey."

I count steps on the way to school—283. School is 283 steps from my house.

When Hallowell High comes into view, I feel fourteen again. It's the first day of school and I'm scared. I'm standing in the middle of the parking lot. Anna bounds over to me and she's excited. It's the first day of school and she's a lowly frosh, but she's ready to take this whole place on. She claimed it as hers before anyone else got the chance, and we gave it to her because she was the only one who looked like she knew what she was doing, and I just went along with it because I didn't know.

I spot her Benz at the front of the school. They're here. I stalk across the pavement to the front doors. My pulse thrums in my ears, a prelude to a panic attack. I grip the door handle and pull it open. It's like my finger on the trigger.

My finger is on the trigger and—

Bang.

The school is quiet. Distant ghost-footsteps reach my ears. I jog up the stairs to the lockers, and there's nothing. I expect journal pages taped to the walls, shoved in lockers, everywhere. But the school looks like it always does.

I don't believe it. It's an illusion of peace. I hurry to my locker and spin the dial. Here. It has to be here. It's not just his torture; it's mine. It takes forever to get the right numbers, my hands are shaking so badly, but I finally get it and I pull the lock off and open my locker and—

Nothing.

But she's here. I saw the Benz. They're here and they're early and they're ruining lives because that's what they'd do. That's what she told me she was going to do.

I check the washroom. The empty changing room. The entire school is mine; it's so early, and I find nothing. How many ways can they do this?

I'm not clever like Anna. I'm missing something important.

The school begins to fill up. I listen to snatches of conversations, hoping for some indication, someone else finding it first, but there's nothing. I wander the halls. It gets busier, busier, busier. The busier it gets, the more bodies I have to contend with.

I glimpse Michael at his locker and he's okay.

I hide while he opens it up and wait for it—*this is it, this has to be it*—but nothing. Nothing happens. He just stands there, and this is any day. A normal day. He pauses, like he knows he's being watched. He does. He looks around. I back into the alcove and count to ninety, and when I look again, he's gone.

The bell rings. I stay in the alcove while the morning announcements start. If it hasn't happened by now, this is a slow build, a painfully slow build to it. Girl-bombs getting ready to go off and leave us all in pieces. I make my way down the hall and push through the door to the girls' washroom and Anna is there, staring at her reflection in the mirror. Her hands are on her makeup bag, but she's not moving. She's just staring at herself.

I back into the door, the handle jamming into purple-yellow-brown skin all over my back. I wince and turn, pulling the door open so I can leave.

"Come to gloat?" she asks.

I let the door handle slip from my grasp, but I keep my back to her and keep my mouth shut. I stare at the fading blue paint on the door, chipping around the edges.

*Come to gloat?*

I don't understand what that means.

"What are you talking about?"

She turns her head and takes me in. Checks me, I know, for remnants of what happened last Friday, but there's nothing she can see from where she's standing and nothing I'm willing to show her. Her eyes search mine, and then she laughs, softly.

"You don't know?"

What don't I know. She went straight to Holt. Michael will leave quietly and without a fight. That's not like her. Public humiliation is way more her style. She had a change of heart? I shake my head slowly.

I don't know.

She unzips her makeup bag and rummages through it, but her

usual morning makeup routine seems lost to her. She starts with the lip gloss usually, but now it feels like she's just looking for something to do with her hands.

"I'm done with you. I'm done with Michael. Your little friend, Liz—" She laughs and shakes her head. "She threatened to go to Holt about what *I* did to you. Hilarious."

The words settle in slow, twisting my stomach. I stare at Anna, my mouth trying to form a reply, but nothing comes out. I don't—I don't believe it.

"But the photocopies—"

"Liz has them and I said I'm done with you." She finally finds the gloss. "Go."

"Just because Liz won't go to Holt now doesn't mean I won't," I tell her. "I can still go to Holt. Show him the bruises."

She drops the gloss back in her bag and I notice she's trembling; she's afraid. She knows I could go to Holt and I'd have her. I would have her.

But I want something better.

"You're scared," I tell her. Anna. Scared. She gives me a look that could kill. "You always said none of this matters, and you're scared."

"It *doesn't* matter," she says tightly. "But it's good practice."

I have never hated anyone so much in my life.

I never will again.

I pull the door open and step out into the hall.

I spend lunch outside, sitting on the front steps numb. Relieved. Alone.

Until Michael comes out.

I know it's him without turning around. He shuts the door carefully and hesitates before sitting next to me, his side brushing against mine. I can't look at him at first.

"Liz told me everything," he says.

And then I know that it's okay.

I press my forehead against his shoulder. He exhales slowly.

It's quiet. Postwar quiet.

Later, we'll try to make sense of this. Eventually, the bruises will fade.

But for now, he reaches over and puts his hand on top of my hand, curling his fingers into the spaces between mine, closing them around my palm until they're laced tightly, locked together, school behind us, and I realize Anna is right.

A whole world exists outside of that hellhole.

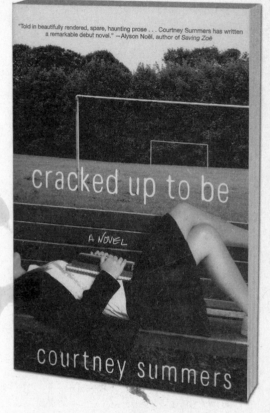